IT'S NOT ABOUT THE KILL

LIFE OF INCREDIBLE JOURNEYS

BY

CY ANGELLOZ

Case ID:
1-14951239201
ISBN:
978-1-968973-72-8
LCCN:
2025914006

Dedication

To all the wonderful clients I was able to work with, helping with their journey into the Great Outdoors.

Dick and Mary Cable - An Incredible Couple that shared all the clients the equipment needed for their Adventures

Acknowledgment

Joyce White is an incredible Editor. I was Blessed to share my life and book with her and watched her transform it into an incredible Book.

Dan Castro, Lawyer and Law Professor, with whom I spent a week while I was learning the Law Side in Realtor Classes,

Dan 15 years ago insisted I write a Book. He said the Title should be (It's Not About the $$$)

About the Author

I consider myself to be one of the luckiest men in the world to spend 45 years of my prime life traveling the world and sharing my father with everyone I came into contact with.

Table of Contents

Introduction

For years, I considered writing this book, but the moment I knew it had to happen was when I finally crossed back into Texas. After spending a decade working for Cabela's Outdoor Adventures in Nebraska as one of their senior consultants, the feeling of being home again was unlike anything else. Texas wasn't just a place—it was where my roots ran deep, where the air itself seemed to welcome me back like an old friend.

My time at Cabela's was a dream career in many ways. I specialized in helping people chase their passions—sending folks around the world to hunt big game, fish in untouched waters, or experience the thrill of wing shooting. I loved connecting people with their adventures, but deep down, I always carried my own stories, shaped by a childhood unlike most.

I was born and raised in Corpus Christi, Texas, along the Gulf Coast. My upbringing was a mix of tradition and unpredictability, shaped by a father who had lived an extraordinary life and a mother who dedicated herself to keeping our family together. I had an older brother and sister, both of whom walked very different paths from mine.

My father had just retired from the Marine Corps when I was born, but before that, he had lived a life of courage and sacrifice. He had flown Corsairs as a Marine pilot, serving in both World War II and the entire Korean conflict. His journey started much earlier than most—at just 15 years old, he began attending LSU, well ahead of his peers. He was already going into his third year of college when the war called to him. Too Young to enlist on his own, his mother had to sign the paperwork allowing him to join early. Even then, the military required enlistees to be at least 18 unless a parent gave their approval. With that signature, he left college behind and joined the Navy, determined to serve his country. He earned his wings and later transitioned into the Marine Corps, where none other than Pappy Boyington—a legendary and highly decorated Marine pilot—signed him off in his flight logs.

He spent so much time overseas during those years that my earliest memory of him wasn't until I was four. By then, he had returned, but his world was still filled with aviation. I remember how he used to take me to the Naval Air Station and leave me at the hangars all day while he worked in his office. For hours, I would watch pilots come and go, sit inside different aircraft, and soak in the sounds and smells of that world. It was an adventure of its own, one that few kids ever got to experience.

My father wasn't just a pilot; he was a brilliant man, a statistician overseeing multiple bases across the Southern U.S. I suppose that's why everyone at the hangar treated me so well; I was the boss's kid. But to me, they weren't just being kind; I felt like I belonged, like I was part of something bigger.

I was the youngest in our family by a stretch. My brother was nine years older than I, and my sister was four years older. I was, as they liked to say, the "accident"—a result of one too many gin and tonics at an officer's ball. My parents always told the story with a laugh, but there was a truth to it.

My mother, whom I loved dearly, was the heart of our home. She embodied the role of a traditional housewife, ensuring we were cared for, meals were prepared, and the house felt like a safe place. She, my father, and my siblings all had their own interests, but there was one thing they never quite understood—my love for the outdoors.

While my family had little to no interest in nature, adventure, or hunting, I was drawn to it as a calling. I found myself captivated by the wild, by the untamed landscapes that stretched beyond the boundaries of everyday life.

Throughout my life, I have traveled to some of the most fascinating places on earth, immersing myself in cultures, wildlife, and the raw beauty of the outdoors. In this book, I have chosen to share stories from the countries that left a lasting imprint on me—places where I faced challenges, experienced joy, and found hope.

As you turn these pages, my wish is for you to feel what I felt—to relive the excitement, the fear, the triumphs, and the lessons that shaped me. Whether you're an adventurer at heart or simply someone looking for a glimpse into a different world, I hope these stories bring you something meaningful.

Because in the end, adventure isn't just about where you go—it's about what you discover along the way.

Chapter 1
Why?

It's time I share with my readers why I decided to write this book.

After spending ten years early in my career with Cabela's Outdoor Adventures in Nebraska, I returned home to Texas with a vision. I wanted to start a small consulting group, obtain my real estate license, and secure my permit to carry.

In the early days of setting up my office, Jimmy Deringer and Louie Schriener from the YO Ranch dropped by to discuss a potential collaboration. At first, I declined. However, a few days later, Louie invited me out to the ranch, informing me that they were hosting a big pachanga with the DSC group from Dallas. I agreed to attend. A week later, at the YO Ranch office in Ingram, I met with Louie, his brother Charlie IV, and their attorney to discuss joining their team.

After three hours of discussion, I agreed to join under two conditions. First, I wanted to take their existing outdoor school for children and expand it into a full-fledged program that would teach kids about hunting, tracking, shooting skills, and everything I had learned growing up. Second, I needed the freedom to continue my other consulting duties outside of the YO Ranch. They agreed, and with that, I became part of their team.

For the next five years, I worked with the YO Ranch, teaching Young boys and girls about the outdoors, wildlife, and conservation. The YO was a well-known high-fence ranch, home to native game and exotics. I fully understood the role of high-fence hunting and its contribution to wildlife conservation.

During this time, I was also working on my real estate license. I had a lawyer, whom I'll call "D," teach me the legal side of real estate. He loved hearing about my adventures and often encouraged me to write a book. In fact, it was D who gave me the idea for this book's title.

And now, twelve years later, I'm finally writing the story. While there are many experiences I will leave out, my focus will remain on the adventures, as well as stories about my father. Over the next several chapters, I will take you through my journey—one that spans a forty-five-year career, covering over 150 countries, 40 trips to Africa, and countless visits to Central America, North America, Canada, and even three expeditions to the Arctic. I have also traveled extensively across South America, New Zealand, Australia, and Mongolia.

In later chapters, I will revisit my time at the YO Ranch and my ten years with Cabela's. But for now, let's get into some adventure stories!

Chapter 2
Tech Years

During my college years, I chose to attend Texas Tech. How did I choose Texas Tech? You're going to love this story.

One summer day in 1971, while preparing to finish up my senior year of high school, I was helping my dad with yard work on a Saturday afternoon in Corpus Christi. My dad turned to me and asked, "Son, have you started thinking about college?"

After I graduated from high school, I said, "Dad, between hunting, fishing, surfing, and chasing girls, I don't think college is my gig."

In the fall of '72, I headed up to Texas Tech in Lubbock, Texas. Back in those days, it was a seven-hour drive from Corpus Christi. That first semester, two friends who had already been there for two years started urging me to join Phi Delta Theta. I didn't know much about fraternities, but they took me to some incredible parties, and I immediately understood why Playboy had rated Texas Tech number one for the best-looking coeds.

It just so happened that the fraternity I joined was mainly composed of jocks, cowboys, and so-called stud muffins. When I showed up at Tech, I drove a van, had a beard, and sported a large Afro. Needless to say, my pledge period and Hell Week were a little rough, but I finally made it in. To make a long story short, by my junior year, I was fully immersed in the college experience.

One day, my dad said, "Son, between you, your brother, and your sister Haye, your mom and I have managed to stay out of trouble."

I replied, "Yes, sir. And I am very appreciative."

He continued, "Well, son, you're going to go to college and get a degree. After that, if you want to be a bum, you're on your own. Am I clear?"

"Yes, sir," I replied.

A few days later, one of my best friends who lived about five houses down invited me over. He was the quarterback of our football team and an incredible athlete. While in his room, I noticed a 1971 Playboy magazine on his bedside table. The cover read: "Best Looking Coeds." When I opened it, in full color, it rated Texas Tech as number one.

A few days later, we were at the dinner table—my mom at one end, my brother and sister across from me, and my dad at the other end. My mom turned to my dad, whom she called "Angie," and asked, "Have you had that talk with your son about college?"

"Yes, we had that talk on Saturday, and he's working on it," my dad replied.

"Good," she said.

"Mom, I've decided I want to go to Tech," I announced.

My mom raised an eyebrow. "Cy, a week ago, you told your dad you didn't even know if you were going to college. How did you come up with Texas Tech?"

"Well, Mom, I just have a good feeling about it."

I thought my brother and sister were going to choke on their food.

A year before I officially declared my intentions, my freshman year was spent as a pre-law student. That summer, I worked at a law firm in Corpus Christi. They were ambulance chasers, and being naive about the legal industry, I quickly realized that was not the path for me. In my sophomore year, I decided to try psychology because my older sibling was a Ph.D. psychologist specializing in adolescent psychology. However, I quickly realized that most of the professors in that field were the ones who needed to be in a rubber room.

Finally, after four and a half years, I earned a Bachelor of Arts and Science degree in Land Use Management.

Chapter 3
Big Game Consulting

In my early years, fresh out of college and before embarking on my consulting career, I was hired to manage a newly developed country club and housing development called Fair Oaks, located just south of Boerne, Texas. The development sat on a sprawling 5,500-acre ranch owned by the Fair family, with Ralph Fair as the owner. When they extended the offer to me, I looked Ralph in the eye and told him bluntly, "I think you're crazier than an acre of snakes." I was flattered by the opportunity, but had to acknowledge the reality—I had just turned 25. However, after some discussion, I agreed on the condition that we reassess after one year to determine if I wanted to pursue a long-term future in the club business. They agreed.

The first four years flew by, keeping me constantly engaged and challenged. I learned a great deal about managing a large operation, overseeing a high-end clientele, and maintaining the intricate balance required to run both the stock and the country club. It was an invaluable period of growth and experience.

During this time, I also made the difficult decision to put an end to my involvement in Mexico Adventures. Spending significant time in Mexico has allowed me to deeply understand the soul of its people and their rich culture. The people, as a whole, were kind and hardworking, but the government, heavily influenced by the cartels, was steadily eroding the country's stability. I witnessed firsthand the impact this corruption had on everyday life, and I knew it was no longer a viable option for my pursuits.

Despite stepping away from certain aspects of adventure travel, my passion for the outdoors never waned. During my time in Mexico, I spent many days hunting mule deer and Coues deer in the western deserts. This was at the beginning of Mexico's rise as a premier destination for mule deer hunting. I vividly remember a few exhilarating hunts guided by the Pima Indians, tracking mule deer across the arid desert floor. The thrill of the hunt, the patience required, and the connection with the land made it an unforgettable experience.

But enough about Central and South America—for now. I'll return later to recount my time fishing for peacock bass in the Amazon tributaries of Brazil.

Back at Fair Oaks, the country club was thriving, and I had come to know our members well. Most were a joy to work with, though some presented unique challenges. During my fourth year managing the club, a meat purveyor visited to showcase different cuts of meat to our head chef. During his visit, he asked if I still enjoyed hunting. I admitted that I did, though I had been too busy to go on a trip recently. That's when he shared with me an intriguing opportunity—an all-inclusive 10-day safari in Zambia. The trip included the chance to hunt one Cape buffalo and seven Plains game species, with all expenses, including airfare and round-trip travel, totaling $5,500. Needless to say, I was very interested.

That evening, I called my friend Tom from Texas Tech. He wasn't a fraternity brother, but we had met at the old Intramural Gym while I was preparing for a boxing tournament. He had asked if he could spar with me, and though I hesitated at first, we ended up having a solid match. We had stayed in touch ever since. When I told Tom about the safari, he didn't hesitate— " Count me in," he said.

The wait for August was agonizing. Both of us were filled with anticipation, and I couldn't shake the feeling that my expectations were set impossibly high. I feared I would be let down. But as we boarded the flight to Zambia, my excitement only grew.

After a grueling 1.5 days of travel, we finally landed and were greeted by our Professional Hunter (PH), Abie Duploy. That afternoon, we embarked on a four-hour drive to the main camp, and I can't begin to describe how deeply the African landscape affected both Tom and me. The vast, untamed wilderness was unlike anything we had ever seen.

Tom had his sights set on a Cape buffalo, while I was after a kudu. By day three, Tom had successfully taken down a magnificent 44-inch Cape buffalo, and on day four, I followed suit with a 48-inch Cape buffalo of my own. Over the following days, we filled our tags with various plains game species. As is always the case with adventures of this magnitude, the days flew by faster than we wanted them to.

Leaving camp was difficult. As we packed our bags and prepared to depart, I found myself wishing I could stay and become a PH in Zambia. The idea of living in the heart of the African bush, guiding hunters, and immersing myself in this extraordinary world was intoxicating.

On the long flight home, I couldn't stop thinking about the trip. It had ignited something deep inside me, and I knew—without a doubt—that I would return. I didn't know when or how, but I made myself a promise: one day, I would become a consultant and help others fulfill their dream adventures.

That first trip to Africa changed the course of my life. Three years later, at the age of 28, I walked away from the country club business and started from the ground up to become a Big Game Consultant. There's no way to fully explain what an incredible life this path has given me.

Since that first adventure, I have returned to the magical continent of Africa 40 times over the last 45 years. In the early days of my consulting career, I made several trips to Central America, mainly for fishing and wing shooting, punctuated by returns to Africa. I also traveled extensively to South America for wing shooting and spent many seasons in Mexico doing the same. However, by the early 1990s, Mexico had become too unsafe, and I knew it was time to shift my focus elsewhere.

The journey that began with one unforgettable safari had evolved into a lifetime of adventure. And the best part? It was only just beginning.

Chapter 4
Lessons in the Shade

Fairly early in my career, I had a very challenging experience with a client that I was going to take to Tanzania. He was a Young man from Louisiana. I had previously sent him and his wife on a few South Texas deer hunts. She was a jewel of a woman. He was a hard-driving Type A personality. Mr. H called me one day and wanted to embark on his first African Safari. I asked him if he wanted to go on what I called a starter safari or head straight into the big safari right out of the box. I knew the answer before I even asked the question, so I decided to send him and his wife on a full-blown 21-day full-bag Safari to Tanzania.

It started out with him and his wife going together, with me accompanying. I figured that with his lovely wife going, it would make it less challenging with personality differences. At this point in my career, I was pretty well seasoned, but not completely seasoned.

There's a lot that goes into building a safari like this. First, you have to select the correct PH (Professional Hunter) to match the client's personality. (Very important — this level of safari is very pricey, and if you don't select a well-seasoned PH with a high profile and the patience of Job, it could end up being a nightmare.)

I chose George Angelides Safari Company in Tanzania and requested Nicky Blunt to be the PH. Nicky was a very well-seasoned British PH and would not let any strong personality break him if you know what I mean.

Clients, no matter how many safaris they end up going on, usually remember their first most vividly. I booked the hunt a year out and stayed in touch with Mr. H very often.

Six months out, I got a call from Mr. H's secretary. She was double-checking the dates. When I reminded her, she informed me that Mr. H couldn't go at that time — he and his wife had planned a trip to Disney World.

I quickly let her know I needed to speak with Mr. H directly, to remind him that this was not like booking a golf match at the country club — they would have to postpone the trip to Walt Disney World. She put Mr. H on the phone. He tried to challenge my decision — that went over like a turd in a punch bowl. After he calmed down, Mr. H came to his senses about two months later, after taking care of that dust-up.

About three months out, Mr. H gave me another call and informed me that his wife was pregnant. I informed him that the doctor was not going to allow her to take the shots required for traveling to Tanzania while pregnant. Mr. H asked if I would still go if she couldn't. Reluctantly, knowing what a challenge it would be, I said yes. That's part of my job — sometimes as challenging as any other part.

Before I proceed, something popped into my mind that I want to share, maybe because it adds a little humor to the life of a consultant. For years, I have always attended DSC and SCI — the two largest hunting conventions in the world.

In my profession, they are a must.

By this time in my career, I had already booked several hundred safaris — from 7-day plains and game starter safaris to full-blown 21-day full-bag trips across nine different countries on the continent of Africa.

Every time a couple would come in to book, it was like watching the next episode of a soap opera. The husband would want to share all about his previous hunting adventures — what he shot, how long it took — it's just part of the process. It's like they want you to know this isn't their first rodeo.

By this point in the conversation, the wife, usually quiet and shy, would chime in with:

"On our last safari, I shot the number four duiker."

There are many species of duikers on the continent of Africa. They are relatively small African antelopes; their horns might average about three inches in length. But the most comical part of the story is that at least ten women have told me they shot the number four duiker in the world! I don't understand why it's always number four, but you make the call.

Finally, Mr. H and I flew into Arusha, Tanzania, and overnighted at the Impala Inn. The next morning, we were picked up by Nicky and chartered to our concession (hunting area).

After about an hour, we arrived at camp.

The staff sighted in Mr. H's gun, and we relaxed that night around the boma, enjoying duiker skewers and beverages.

I always ask my clients to bring some old ball caps to give to the staff — I always bring about a dozen myself. We would pass out each other's caps; I would act like I wanted one of his, and he would want one of mine. By the end of the night, we had more than enough caps for the staff.

The next morning, we got up early and started hunting. Mr. H was being very much Mr. H — he had a plan, a schedule in his head, and felt like he was under a stopwatch. For the first seven days, we averaged about two species a day, taking good trophies. Nicky and I tolerated Mr. H's enthusiasm and fully understood his excitement.

On Day 7, we parked under the shade of a very large acacia tree. Nicky laid out a blanket, and we were enjoying lunch. At some point, Mr. H looked at me and said, "Cy, what are you going to do when you retire?" I was probably 36 at the time.

I said, "Mr. H, I don't focus on that. I'm living life now. You and I have no guarantee we'll even be here tomorrow."

Mr. H said, "Cy, I'm being serious with you. I'm sure you don't make a lot of money."

I said, "Mr. H, I make enough to get by, and I'm so pleased that I have a job I love."

I added, "I've hunted with a lot of very wealthy men and women, and in most cases, they see my job and are envious."

Mr. H, being a Type A go-getter, just couldn't let it go. He started at me again.

I stopped him and said,

"Mr. H, can I ask you a few questions?"

He said, "Sure, fire away."

I asked, "Mr. H, what are you doing this very instant?"

He said, "I'm in Tanzania on a 21-day safari with you and Nicky."

Nicky was sitting right behind him, grinning.

I asked, "When you get back, what's your favorite car to drive?"

He answered, "My black Suburban."

I said, "Let's say you have a nice house with a good roof, bedrooms, kitchen, living room, dining room, etc."

Mr. H, a little perturbed, said, "Cy, where are you going with this?"

I said, "Mr. H, right now I'm on a 21-day safari with you and Nicky.

When I get home, I'll drive my Tahoe.

And my house has everything your house has — probably not as large and far less expensive — but all the creature comforts of home." About that time, Nicky said,

"Guys, lunch is over — we have some more critters to look for."

In my adventure travels, I've always tried to learn some of the local language — basic greetings like hello, good morning, good night, thank you, and you're welcome. We were a little more than halfway through the safari, and Mr. H had refused to say a single word in Swahili (to each his own).

But on about Day 12, when Mr. H and I were having breakfast in the mess tent, he looked at me and said,

"Cy, do you feel okay?"

I said, "For the last couple of days, my stomach has been upset. I think it's the malaria meds."

He said, "You should have told me — I have a pill for that.

He ran back to his tent to get it.

When he returned, he tried to explain to the Black staff that I had a stomach cramp — but he scrambled his Swahili and accidentally said something much worse.

In Swahili, "Tumbo" means stomach. Whatever he said, the staff flew out of that tent like they were launched on rockets. If you don't find that funny, I can't help you.

Well, the 21-day safari eventually came to a close. Mr. H said the only animal he didn't get was a lion, although he did get to see a few male lions come to bait — none of which were mature enough to take.

The next morning, after seeing Mr. H off, I took a taxi down to the Mt. Meru Hotel.

I wanted to find a good driver to take me to the Ngorongoro Crater — a place I had yet to visit, one of the most famous geological destinations in the world.

After visiting with a few drivers, I found one with a gentleness that I liked. It was about a two-hour drive from Arusha to the crater. My driver spoke understandable English, though he was a Muslim man born and raised in Tanzania (very common). On the drive, I asked him, "Why do you think God put this unique geological structure in Africa, and right here in Tanzania?"

We had an excellent conversation. I could tell he was really thinking about it. We had a great day at the crater, got back that afternoon, and the next day I flew back home to Texas. What could have been a very difficult adventure turned out to be incredible.

It was my Father's plan.

Chapter 5
Brazil Fishing

Cabela first called me up to interview for a consulting position in 1995 while I was still working with the YO Group. Before heading up there in late May, I didn't even tell my partners. I knew it would be difficult for Louie, especially to understand, and I wasn't sure I would even take the offer.

I decided to drive up because I wanted to see how long the trip would be. I arrived, as best as I can remember, on a Monday and went to the Cabela's store in Sidney. Back then, Outdoor Adventures was on the second floor of the main store. At that time, they had a GM and two other consultants.

As soon as I got upstairs, I immediately ran into Russell Selle, a consultant I had known for years in the business.

I closed by saying, "I feel the way you guys do—I'm not into High Fence either, but it's going to become a big part of hunting in the future, whether you like it as a company or not."

We broke for lunch and came back afterward, picking up where we left off.

We got back into that conversation after lunch, and they asked me if I had clients who were involved with that style of hunting. I replied yes and explained that many big, serious worldwide hunters are also collectors of species. On some of the HF ranches, they can collect species that don't even exist anymore in some countries where they were once prolific.

Eventually, they came around and said I had made a good point, but they did not want to advertise that style of hunting.

The Fly Fishing School took about six months, and I learned fast. My first fishing destination was Brazil, where I traveled to fish for Peacock Bass in the tributaries of the Amazon.

On that trip, I left from the main airport in Denver, Colorado, about an hour and forty-five minutes from my office in Sidney, NE. It was a fairly new airport at that time, and it was a big one.

I flew to Miami and met up with twenty of the clients I would be fishing with for a week in Brazil. It was a mixture of couples and a couple of single men, mainly in their sixties and seventies. At that time, I was in my late thirties. We caught a mid-morning flight, first landing in Aruba for refueling, and then continuing to Manaus, Brazil.

On the flight, I went around introducing myself and got to know a little about most of them. While in Aruba refueling, we were in the duty-free shop, and I bought a box of Cuban cigars. One of the party, an older Jewish attorney, came up and asked if I was going to make a purchase. He asked if I was buying a whole box, and I replied yes. He said, "Those are awfully expensive." I told him, "I'm normally very conservative, but occasionally, I will treat myself because I enjoy a good cigar." He replied, "Whatever," and later, I learned he was a big-time attorney in his day and was actually a player in the O.J. Simpson trial.

We journeyed on to Manaus, Brazil, with our gear to the bass boats provided, traveled to the land-based camp that night, and settled into our bungalows.

The next morning, we were paired with a boat and headed out to fish for Peacock Bass. I got paired up with a gentleman who, a few years earlier, I had sent to Quebec, Canada, for Quebec Labrador Caribou.

That morning, we got off to a rough start. He obviously never spent much time with a bait-casting reel, and I spent most of my morning helping him get the bird's nest out of his reel—that's what you call a backlash. We caught a few basses, and I quickly found they were just as powerful as I had been told. Luckily, before I left, the Cabela's team had fixed me up with indestructible lures. They had to put in stronger treble hooks and used super glue when they replaced the hooks.

You can't imagine how powerful they are. We would also occasionally catch Payara and Piranha. Believe it or not, I had some very interesting conversations in the evening.

We would all sit outside at a long table with ten of us to a side, with tiki torches for light. I can remember the Peacock Bass being delightful table fare.

Every night after dinner, I would bring out a cigar and always offer one to the old Jewish lawyer. Every night, he would say, "No, thank you. Those are way too expensive." But he would tell me on the flight back that he would present me with a surprise.

Every night, there was an older gentleman sitting across from me. He didn't talk very much, but I felt like I knew him. On about the third night, I said, "I finally figured out who you remind me of."

He said, "Who's that?"

As the trip came to a close and we boarded our flight home, we made one final stop in Aruba. It was a Sunday morning, and the casinos were putting on lavish buffets. As we strolled toward a nearby bar for a cocktail, the old attorney walked ahead of me, casually picking snacks from the buffet the entire way.

He took a seat beside me at the bar and began recounting stories from his past. Back in the late '40s, he said, he had been heavily involved in horse racing and even owned a few remarkable thoroughbreds. At his very first race at Pimlico, he was invited up to the exclusive Jockey's Bar, reserved for the elite. While enjoying his first drink there, he happened to glance up and notice a row of light green Foot Lockers overhead.

As he continued, the attorney pulled out a cigar holder and offered me one of the cigars. The moment I held it, I could tell it was incredibly fresh, like it had just been rolled. He explained it was a pre-Castro Cuban cigar, decades old but astonishingly well-preserved. I instinctively began to prepare it my usual way, licking the outer leaf. The attorney immediately stopped me, grabbing my hand with mild alarm.

Apparently, he didn't approve of my technique.

I looked at him and said, "Excuse me, Counselor—did you just give me this cigar?"

He nodded, still puzzled.

"Then I believe I'm allowed to prepare it how I see fit."

He paused, then said, "You're holding a $5,000 cigar."

"Counselor, I know you can't buy cigars like this anymore," I said, examining it with new respect. "But if I could, what would one like this go for today?" The attorney pulls out a cigar holder, he hands me one of the cigars, and I can tell by feeling it that it feels as fresh as if it has just been made.

This is a pre-Castro cigar, which is very old, but it felt like a brand-new cigar. I started to lick the cigar, and the attorney grabbed my hand. He did not agree with my style of preparing a cigar before lighting it.

I looked at the attorney and said, "Excuse me, counselor, did you give me this cigar?" and he had a puzzled look on his face and replied, "Yes". And his reply was, " You are smoking a $5000 cigar."

"Councilor, I know you can't buy cigars like this anymore". And if I could buy a cigar like this one, what would be the current value?"

Chapter 6
Polar Bear

Polar bear hunting is ranked among the world's top big-game hunts, along with tiger hunting (now fully protected), elephant hunting, and the pursuit of Marco Polo sheep, to name a few. This was one of the last major bookings I handled before Cabela's hired me to join their staff in Nebraska.

Up to this point in my career, I had already booked and personally hunted most of the North American species. One day, I received a call from a Mexican national named Mr. G, whom I had hunted with a few times during my tenure at the YO Ranch.

Mr. G called and said, "Mr. Cy, I want to go shoot a polar bear."

I replied, "Mr. G, are you sure? This is a serious endeavor. A polar bear hunt can be extremely demanding, both physically and mentally. It's bitterly cold, and the Arctic landscape is unforgiving."

Without hesitation, Mr. G said, "Mr. Cy, let's book the hunt."

From the moment we finalized the booking, I spent considerable time preparing him for the adventure, going over every detail meticulously.

About two months before the hunt, Mr. G called me. "Mr. Cy," he said, "My wife and I are expecting our first baby."

"That's great! Congratulations!" I replied.

He then followed up with, "Mr. Cy, I've heard that polar bears are very dangerous. Also, I'm Mexican, and Mexicans don't like cold weather."

Sensing where this was going, I asked, "What are you trying to tell me?"

"Mr. Cy, I need to back out of this hunt."

At this point, I had to inform him, "Mr. G, I'm afraid I can't get you any money back. You've already invested $30,000."

To my surprise, Mr. G responded, "Mr. Cy, I'm not worried about the money." There was a pause before he continued, "Will you do me a favor? Will you go up and shoot my polar bear for me?"

I asked, "Mr. G, are you serious?"

He confirmed, "Yes, Mr. Cy. I'll cover all your expenses, including airfare."

Prior to this offer, I had hunted Central Ground Caribou and Musk Ox in the Arctic, but this was a whole new level of adventure.

Before I knew it, I was packing for my polar bear hunt. I left the next morning, and my first stop was in the Northwest Territories (NWT). After overnighting there, I caught a small charter flight to Igloolik, a remote northern village.

Upon arrival, I met with the wildlife officers, signed the necessary legal documents, and was shuttled to my accommodations—a modest yet comfortable double-wide motel.

The next morning, I met the Inuit driver who would take me to my guide. He pulled a kamatik—a long wooden sled with a wooden box in the center—behind a snowmobile. I couldn't understand his language, but we communicated through gestures. The journey to meet my guide (Nat) took three days and two nights, including one night spent in a two-man igloo due to a sudden whiteout.

On my first night in Igloolic, I was greeted by a friendly Canadian missionary couple. The husband was a dentist who provided dental care for the local Inuit people. They invited me over to their home, and we caught up on world events. They were extremely hospitable and gave me a fascinating insight into the indigenous culture.

The next morning, I set out on my journey to meet Nat. My driver had no radio, compass, or any means of communication with the outside world.

On the first day, the weather seemed perfect—clear blue skies and an endless white landscape stretching in every direction. Later in the afternoon, my driver suddenly stopped, walked back to the kamatik, and grabbed a handsaw. Though the weather seemed fine to me, he began walking around, pressing his heels into the snow. Then, without warning, he started cutting blocks of snow and ice, building an igloo.

In less than an hour, he had constructed a small but functional igloo that we could both fit inside. Just as he packed the last handful of snow into the final crack, the wind picked up, and we found ourselves in a complete whiteout.

We spent the night inside, and when we woke up—what I assumed was morning—we packed up the kamatik and continued on our way. Around midday, we came across two men heading back from a hunt. They were from Austria and spoke broken English. When they removed their snow masks, their faces looked like they had been scalded with hot oil.

I asked what had happened, and they explained that, on their first day, they had removed their masks for just a couple of hours, and the Arctic sun had literally fried their skin—lesson number one.

I then asked if they had been cold during their time in the field. They admitted they had been miserably cold the entire trip. When I asked if they had changed their inner clothing daily, they said no—lesson number two.

In these extreme conditions, it's crucial to swap out your underclothing for dry layers every day, or the trapped moisture will make you dangerously cold.

After saying our goodbyes, we continued on our journey. A couple of hours later, it started snowing—not a blizzard, but steady snowfall. At one point, my driver stopped, retrieved his rifle, and began firing at an animal in the distance. However, he wasn't hitting his target.

I took my rifle, aimed carefully, and brought the animal down. As we approached, I realized it was a juvenile caribou. We field-dressed the caribou and continued on our way.

That night, we stayed in what I would describe as a rudimentary goat hunter's shed. The next morning, we set out again under bright blue skies, with miles and miles of white stretching out in all directions.

About three hours into our journey, I noticed some objects on the ground in the distance. As we got closer, I saw what appeared to be two people standing on a large mound of snow, about ten feet high.

When we reached them, they barely acknowledged me. I got off the komatik and attempted to climb up the snow mound. Every time I tried, I slid back down. You can't imagine how difficult it is to climb a ten-foot mound in a bulky caribou-hide suit, complete with a face mask and all the necessary Arctic gear.

On my third attempt, I finally made it to the top. The older man at least extended his hand to help me up.

This was just the beginning of my polar bear adventure.

At this time, I was standing on top of a large mound of ice and snow when my guide, Nat, called my name.

"This is my son, George," Nat said. Then, the next words out of his mouth were, "Do you want a polar bear?"

I nodded. "That's why I'm here."

Nat pointed to two polar bears about 300 yards away, a sow and a boar. Then he asked, "Do you want two polar bears?"

I shook my head. "No, just one."

I lifted my binoculars to get a better look, but Nat grabbed them while they were still around my neck so he could see for himself. It was a little awkward, but we made it work.

"Let's go," Nat said.

I grabbed my rifle while he got the dogs and sled ready. By law, we couldn't use motorized vehicles for hunting. We traveled about three miles before catching up with the bear. As we closed in, Nat began cutting the leather leads on four of the 15 to 20 dogs. The moment the dogs were released, they charged after the bear, and all hell broke loose.

When the bear was finally bayed, we walked up to within ten feet. I aimed and placed a 300-grain .340 round behind its shoulder. The bear collapsed with all four legs splayed out, but despite the mortal shot, it still swung its head back and forth, letting out a growl that would send chills down anyone's spine.

I reloaded, ready to fire again. Meanwhile, Nat walked up to the bear's back end and placed his hand on its small tail.

"Back away!" I warned him.

Nat turned, looked at me, and calmly said, "I'm Inuit."

I had my rifle ready for a second shot and thought to myself, This man is crazy.

The bear was close to ten feet long and probably weighed around 1,000 pounds. After it finally expired, Nat began skinning it.

As he worked, I looked around for his son and the driver. They were off in the distance, walking carefully on the ice, looking for good spots to cut. That's when it hit me— I was in for another night in an igloo with three other men.

I was wrong. It ended up being three days and two nights.

After we all crawled into the igloo, Nat started preparing polar bear meat for supper. At one point, he asked his son to step outside and grab something. When he returned, he carried a large chunk of walrus meat, already growing green moss on it.

I watched as they prepared it, then reached over to cut myself a piece. But Nat quickly grabbed my hand.

"No," he mumbled. "You get sick and shit."

I took his advice.

The three days were long. I spent my time reading by the light of the Bunsen burner. On the first night, I was reading a book about Armageddon when I felt someone staring at me. I looked up—it was Nat.

"Do you know God?" I asked.

Without hesitation, he replied, "Yes."

I tried to explain what my book was about, but he looked puzzled. So, I asked if he wanted me to read aloud. He nodded.

We mainly survived on saltine crackers and dried whale blubber. Nat would occasionally make hot tea.

On the morning of the third day, the men knocked on the igloo door and started preparing for our journey back. When I stepped outside, the blizzard was still raging.

Nat crawled back in after about an hour, his gloves cradling a small, snow-white rat. I reached out to touch it, but he pulled my hand away.

"No," he said. "Moisture kills."

A strange thought crossed my mind. Three days ago, I had killed a 1,000-pound polar bear, and yet here was Nat, tenderly caring for this tiny white rat.

Read that again and think it through—there's a special lesson about hunters who must hunt to survive.

The trip back was long. When Nat dropped me off at my motel, he asked, "Would you like to hunt seals with me tomorrow?"

I politely declined, and I could see the disappointment in his eyes.

"If I don't go, what will you do?" I asked.

"Hunt seals," he replied.

As he was about to leave, I asked him what time he'd head out. Nat instinctively looked at his left wrist, as if he had a watch—he didn't.

"Ten o'clock," he said.

The next morning, at exactly 10:00 AM, I heard the roar of Nat's snowmobile outside my motel. I hopped on, and off we went.

The excursion lasted about two hours. The area looked like a vast, white football field, with a stretch of flowing water in the middle—about 40 yards long and 20 yards wide.

We sat down at the edge of the ice, watching for seals. Every so often, a seal's head would pop up. When I was ready, I took a shot—but missed, the bullet skimming just over the seal's head.

I knew my rifle was dead on at 100 yards, so when another seal appeared, I adjusted my aim and fired again. Another miss.

I turned to look at Nat. He was rolling on the ground, laughing his ass off.

Frustrated, I walked over, and he drew a picture in the snow—a ball representing the seal's head. Then, he made an indentation two inches above it and pointed.

"Shoot here," he said.

It made no sense to me, but I tried it anyway. The next seal popped up, I aimed two inches above its head and fired. Bullseye.

From then on, we went five for five. After about two hours of hunting, we loaded the seals onto the sled and headed back.

Before Nat left, he invited me to meet his family and have some seals for dinner the next day.

Early the next morning, my dentist—yes, my dentist—came to pick me up. We rode around the village, taking in the sights. At one point, we passed a local indoor gym filled with kids playing sports, from toddlers to teenagers.

"Most of these kids won't make it to adulthood," the dentist said.

I was shocked. "Why?"

"The drugs and alcohol here… It's killing them," he replied.

That was hard to hear.

Later that afternoon, I went to visit Nat's family. As soon as I walked in, I found myself in their living room. There were about eight people in total, including Nat and his wife. Four of them were sitting on the couch, while others sat on the floor.

I'd be remiss if I didn't share what it's like to hunt a wild polar bear in the Arctic.

Growing up, most of us have seen polar bears in movies, magazines, or maybe even at the zoo. But trust me, seeing them in their natural habitat—out there in the Arctic—is something else. They are so majestic, so powerful, that it takes your breath away.

I had hunted wildlife for years. If I could have walked away from harvesting that bear, I would have. But I had made a promise to my client. And besides, when you're that close to a wild polar bear, there is no Plan B. If you hesitate, he will kill you—and eat you.

Chapter 7
China

One year before I departed The YO Group, Louie called me and said, "I got a call from Bob, and he asked me if you could fly to China and help their government with wildlife conservation issues. You know Bob does a lot of business with China."

I said, "Louie, you know the kids' hunting camps are getting ready to kick off this season, and I would rather be here for that."

Louie, in an almost pleading voice, said, "Cy, you know Bob does a lot of business with the ranch, and we can't let him down. He is really counting on this."

I told Louie I would call Bob on Monday. On Monday, I called Bob and said, "Louie informed me you would like me to go to China and help their government officials with their wildlife issues."

Bob's reply was, "Thank you. I have you a flight booked, flying out of San Francisco this Friday at 3:45 on Air China."

You guessed it—I was going to China.

That week, I went through my checklist preparing for the trip. By this time in my travels, I had a pretty well-planned routine.

When I boarded the plane, I found my seat on the right side of the plane. It was a three-seat configuration. I had an aisle seat, and there was already an old Chinese grandmother and a three-year-old grandbaby in the other seats.

I always board an international flight in my civvies and then change into a jogging suit and put on tennis shoes. Back in my seat, I settled in for what was to be a 14-hour flight to Shanghai and then a short hop to Beijing.

After the flight took off, I ordered a glass of red wine. About 30 minutes after takeoff, they served food. I opened the box, and it did not appeal to me.

Forty minutes into the flight, I took a Halcion (a sleeping pill) so I could get some good rest. I usually fall asleep within 30 minutes, but for some reason, I was still wide awake. I figured the pharmacist had given me a lighter dosage, so I took a second. At that point, we were 12 hours out.

I woke up when the wheels were touching down in Shanghai. I looked down at my jogging jacket, a light beige color. I had pee on it, barf on it, animal crackers, and baby sputum. I even had areas on my chest where the baby apparently tried to nurse me.

It was disgusting, but what the heck.

We lifted off for a short flight to Beijing. Upon deboarding, I walked down the plane onto the second floor of the airport, and it looked like a giant red ant bed. I'm thinking, "How is my interpreter going to find me?" I had met him once before at the ranch in Texas with Bob. His name was Wang. In the crowd, waving his hand and calling my name, was Wang.

I met up with Wang and his staff at baggage claim. We went through the meet-and-greet necessities and headed outside, crawling into a government limo. It was a short drive to the Beijing Sheraton, a beautiful, tall hotel in the middle of downtown.

We proceeded up to my room, which was full of fresh flowers, fruit and snack baskets, champagne, and wine iced down.

It made me feel like I was some kind of special dignitary from the USA, and I was just a Bubba from Texas.

Wang spent about an hour going over the itinerary for the next three weeks. Before he left my room, he informed me that his staff would be there the next morning to show me the sights of Beijing.

The next morning, I felt like I was coming down with a possible cold, so I took some cold medication.

The day was interesting. We toured the Great Wall of China, the Forbidden City, and many other tourist sites.

While touring the city all day, I noticed I didn't see any dogs, cats, or lizards, and it registered in my head. It came into play later.

That night, Wang showed up and took me to his favorite Peking duck restaurant next to Tiananmen Square. When we entered the restaurant, I was the only non-Chinese person in the room. We sat down and placed an order. Looking around,

I noticed the folks eating all of the ducks, including the head, beak, feet, and all. It was quite amazing.

We had our meal, and it was incredible. I just ate the main body of the duck, and the folks around me probably thought I was weird.

The next morning, I met with Wang for breakfast at the hotel, and then we were off to the airport to catch a flight to north-central China. We flew on a Russian airline (Aeroflot). Again, I was the only American on the flight of about 30 passengers. Wang informed me we would be flying into a remote airport in Henan and that there probably wouldn't be many people there.

He was wrong. The townspeople must have caught wind that an American was flying in.

When I looked out the flight window at the airport's glass window from floor to ceiling, all I could see was Chinese people from floor to ceiling. I felt like an animal in a zoo on display.

We shot into the little town, and they had prepared a meeting room to go over instructions. There must have been 30 men in the room. The Chinese went over many topics all day.

They informed me we would be traveling south over the next couple of weeks and would end up at the northern tip of Tibet.

They mentioned that outsiders had never been exposed to these areas in China, and occasionally, I would be able to discuss things with them. They mentioned they would take two rifles, and if I saw an animal I would like to take, I could shoot one or two.

That night, they had a special dinner for me and the traveling team. I saw and ate food I never knew existed, like bull penis soup, fish eye soup, monkey balls, and the like.

After dinner, the guys kept wanting me to toast with them. The fluid in the drinks tasted like double-A jet fuel, and they loved it.

By night, I was going downhill fast (sick), so I excused myself and went to bed.

The next morning, we started on our journey, not feeling good but still travel-worthy. That first evening, we went as far as Dulon. I was familiar with it because I had sent hunters for blue sheep and Maral stags. We stayed in yurts that night (Mongolian round tents). That first evening, they took me up on horses and showed me hundreds of wild blue sheep.

The next day, we went further south to a small community in the middle of nowhere. I was feeling so bad and went to my host. On a sanitary level of one to ten, it was about two.

The 10x10 room had a bed with about five mattresses, a wrought-iron frame, and a wire coming down with a light bulb dropping from a 12-foot ceiling. I took more cold medication and got into bed. I would go from burning up to freezing. It was like I had malaria. I fell asleep or passed out from a high fever, and at one point, I felt a cold hand on my forehead. I opened my eyes, and it was Wang. He said, "You are burning up. I'm going to get a doctor."

A few minutes later, an old stereotypical Fu Manchu doctor walked in with an old box in his hand...In the room were the doctor, Wang, and the Provincial Governor. Wang said the doctor wanted me to take off my shirt so he could check my vitals. I did, and I remember the Provincial Secretary staring at the cross I had around my neck. It didn't register at the time.

The doctor checked my vitals, had a chat with Wang, and then Wang informed me that they were going to have to give me some medicine. I said go ahead. He then informed me they would have to administer it internally. I said, "Before you all stick a needle in me under these conditions, I have to see that they're sterile."

A few minutes later, a small nurse walked in. She was so short I could barely see her head beside my bed. She brought two very long bottle vials of a clear liquid, some tubing, and two sterile needles in sealed packages. They wired the two vials to the bedpost with coat hangers and put the needles into the tubing. The nurse was trying to stick the needles into my veins on the top of my hand, and after about three attempts, I grabbed them and stuck them into two veins myself. I was immediately out.

The next morning, when I woke up, a glimmer of light was coming through the window, and birds were starting to chirp. I looked up at the vials, both empty, and pulled the needles and tubes out of my hand. Within a few minutes, Wang and the doctor showed up.

After the doctor checked me out, they asked if I wanted to turn back. I said absolutely not, and Wang informed me the doctor was going to travel with us. I was so weak that they had to assist me out of bed and walk me to one of the Land Rovers. We traveled in these Land Rovers, nine of us in total.

Over the next three days, we were mainly in the Xingzi Range and the Shenmyinlei Mountains. I was seeing wildlife; I thought I had seen everything that had come off Noah's Ark. Every time we stopped to view animals, the Chinamen would run to the back of a Land Rover and pull out rifles. After the third time, I asked Wang to tell his staff that we were there to protect wildlife, not shoot it. I told him that of all the animals I had been viewing, I couldn't even get them back into America.

At one point in the Shee-my-Lei Range, I spotted a couple of rock grouse (wild birds). I asked Wang to have his men bring me the old single-shot .22 rifle. I shot the grouse, and the men went wild with excitement.

After making it to the Tibet border, we started a long trek back. We traveled along the Yangtze River for a distance. When we reached halfway back, we stopped in a small community called Goldmud. We pulled into a four-story motel/hotel that was probably constructed in the '50s. Wang put my gear in my room on the second floor—no elevators, just stairs. We had been traveling for about 12 days at this point. We hadn't bathed, shaved, nothing.

As Wang was leaving my room, he informed me the guys had a party arranged for me in the basement and told me to hurry up. I said, "Wang, I need to clean up and start writing some more notes in my journal." He said he would give me 30 minutes. Later, he was knocking at my door. He said the guys were excited and wanted my presence in the basement.

We walked down to the basement, and it was like walking into an old ballroom. You might have seen growing up—wooden floors, a sparkling ball hanging from the center of the room, and an old, dusty mirrored bar at one end, playing old ballroom music from the '40s.

On one side of the ballroom, in metal chairs, were the men I had been traveling with. On the other side of the room were about 12 women—Geji women, kind of like Geisha girls, you see in Japan. They were all dressed up in their ceremonial gowns, looking like China dolls. Wang walked over to me and said, "All these women are for You."

I said, "Wang, we are not going there."

Wang said, "The guys will be disappointed."

I said, "Wang, during the course of this trip, You guys converse daily about what I am explaining—situations and answers to You. As you know, I don't have a clue what you all are discussing. Would you say they are pleased?"

He said, "Yes, very much so. They have been communicating with the top brass, so when we get back to Beijing in two days, they have prepared a contract for you to sign that basically says future hunts in China will have to go through you."

I said, "We will deal with that meeting in two days. Let the guys know their guest wants to put all our chairs in the middle of the room in a circle under that sparkling ball. We're going to go boy-girl-boy-girl. Let them know I am from America, and I am free to answer any questions they have—that's what it's all about."

He talked to the guys. I could see the look on their faces. It was as if they thought, "If that's what Cy wants to do, we will do it." We circled up the chairs and started the questions and answers at 9:00 PM, and by 1:00 AM, we had completed the full circle. I looked at Wang and said, "I'm out of gas. I have to go to bed."

Chapter 8
Whispers of the Wild

Secrets of Cameroon's Untamed Jungle

I was in my sixth year working with Dr. P, Olivia's dad, and had already booked him on a few of his adventures.

Before I continue, I want to say that Dr. P and I were completely different, yet I had grown to truly love and admire him.

Pete was an electrophysiologist—a heart doctor who specializes in the electrical system of the heart. Trust me, they are highly specialized and have to be absolute brainiacs.

As I recall, I was at an SCI Convention when Dr. P walked into my booth. He sat down and said, "Cy, I think I want to hunt in Cameroon, Central Africa. It's also considered part of Equatorial Africa."

By that point in his hunting journey, Dr. P had already been to Africa about three times. I responded, "Dr. P, let's talk about this tonight at the Paris Hotel." He agreed.

That night, Olivia and I met her dad and one of his doctor friends at the Paris Hotel. Over a round of wine, I said, "Dr. P, I know you've been on a few hunts in Africa, but hunting in Equatorial Africa is a completely different experience from your other trips."

"I'm not sure you're ready for that just yet."

Dr. P looked at me, surprised. "You're not going to book me?"

"Dr. P, I'm not saying that," I reassured him. "But you need to understand what it entails."

We had another glass of wine, and then our dinner was served. As we were leaving, I said, "Come see me in the morning, and we'll discuss this Cameroon hunt further."

The next morning, Dr. P showed up at my booth as soon as the convention floor opened.

I asked, "Dr. P, what's the main antelope you're after?" I was testing him to see if he had done his research.

His answer: "A big bongo."

Then he paused and said, "Cy, if I book this hunt, will you go with me?"

I replied, "Dr. P, if that's the condition, I will—but only under certain terms."

Dr. P grinned, and I proceeded to tell him about the other species he could expect to harvest.

"You can also take dwarf buffalo, red river hogs, western sitatunga, and at least two to four duikers. I think there are nine total in the forest—the yellow-backed duiker, which is the largest, as well as blue, red-flanked, Peters, Gaboon, and Ogilby's duikers."

As I listed more species he might encounter, his smile just grew bigger. Dr. P had reached that stage in his African hunting adventures where he wanted to collect everything that had stepped off Noah's Ark.

After going over the list, which is a common obsession for wealthy hunters once they catch the "Africa bug," I took him to meet the PH (professional hunter) he would be hunting with. I was going to accompany him as an observer to help out, and by this point in my career, I had lost much of my excitement for new species.

Back at the booth, I said, "Dr. P, we're going in May. The jungle is going to be hot and humid. Everything in the bush will stick to you and pull you every which way but loose. And the bugs? Many of them bite, sting, and will make you miserable."

"When we go in and out of Douala, just smile and let the PH and me handle the talking and paperwork." He didn't quite understand why yet, but he would later.

Between booking Dr. P's trip and preparing for the flight to Cameroon, I called him about once a week to get him as ready as possible.

Dr. P was a brilliant man, but nothing could have prepared him for what he was about to experience.

May arrived quickly, and we met at Dulles International in Washington to catch our flight to Cameroon.

The flight went smoothly, and by the next day, we were landing in Douala. I'd been in nicer airports, but it was functional. Dr. P, however, looked a little starstruck.

We got through immigration without any hiccups, and our driver took us to our charter for the flight into the jungle. These charters were reliable and used daily to transport loggers into the forest.

Upon arrival, the staff picked us up at the airstrip and took us to camp. After they unloaded our equipment into our separate tents, we headed to the Boma for some cocktails.

At the Boma, we met two Russian men accompanied by a beautiful female escort. That night, we all had dinner in the mess hall, which thankfully had air conditioning—otherwise, we would have been dripping sweat into our meals.

The next morning, we headed out with the PH and the pygmy trackers. Around midday, we jumped a bongo but couldn't get on it. The forest was so dense that you had to be almost on top of an animal to see it.

On the second day, the dogs bayed two different bongos, but we still couldn't get a shot.

Keep in mind that this was a twelve-day hunt. Returning to camp that evening, I could see that Dr. P was discouraged.

As we stepped out of the Land Rover, I said, "Dr. P, go take a shower and cool off. I'll come to your tent—I have something to show you."

Thirty minutes later, I went to Dr. P's tent. "Dr. P, bring your camera," I said.

He looked at me curiously. "Where are we going?"

"We're taking a little walk."

Earlier, while Pete was taking a shower, I had spoken to the PH, who told me about a nearby Pygmy village. He drew me a small map and explained it was about a 30-minute walk to the west. "There's a good path," he said. "When you cross the little wooden bridge over the stream, you'll almost be there." Before I left, he made me promise to be back before dark.

Dr. P and I walked for about 20 minutes before reaching the bridge. As we stood there, he suddenly grabbed my hand. "Cy, are you proud of me?"

The question caught me off guard. "Dr. P, I'm very proud of you," I assured him. "I told you before this hunt that it would be challenging, but you're holding up well."

As we arrived at the Pygmy camp, the tribal chief, who was also our main tracker, greeted us. Using a mix of gestures and the few words we shared in common, I asked if I could bring my father-in-law into the camp to take a few pictures. He smiled and nodded his approval.

Walking into the village, I felt an odd sense of unease, not fear, just an awareness that this was unlike any other native camp I had ever visited. And by this point in my career, I had been in many across Africa.

The Pygmies lived in small dome-shaped huts made from long leaves draped over bent branches. Everything was built to scale for the small people who lived there. As we approached, we saw women squatting on the ground, wearing only loincloths around their hips, boiling meat in small pots over open fires outside their huts.

Little children, timid and curious, approached us cautiously. We handed them candy, and their faces lit up with wide smiles. Flies clung to their eyes, noses, and lips, and their small bodies were covered in dirt. Most of them were completely naked, playing with crude toys made from sticks.

Dr. P was thoroughly immersed in the moment, taking pictures and playfully rubbing the tops of the children's heads. After a while, he turned to me and said, "We need to head back—it's getting late, and we don't want to be in the jungle after dark."

On the walk back, we didn't exchange a word until we reached the wooden bridge. I stopped and turned to him.

"Dr. P, I've known you for about three years now, and I know you're a deeply spiritual man. What you saw back there—those children, that village—was no accident. By God's choice, you and I were born and raised in the wealthiest country in the world. Your parents had the love and financial means to send you to the finest universities and medical schools in America. And through your hard work and dedication, you became one of the top doctors in your field."

I paused, letting the words sink in before continuing.

"The life you have—Your ability to travel and experience adventures like this—it's all a blessing. But just think... God could have just as easily placed us in that jungle, growing up like those Pygmies. Instead, He had a different plan for us."

I saw tears welling in Dr. P's eyes as I went on. "We're going to get the animals you came here for. But when you wake up tomorrow morning, I want to see you in a good mood. I want to see you having fun. This is the trip of a lifetime, and I won't accept anything less."

Dr. P pulled me into a hug. "Thank You, Cy. This is one of the most memorable conversations I've ever had. I'm sorry if I've been off."

I shook my head. "Dr. P, I didn't say this expecting an apology. But when you lay your head down tonight, I hope you take a moment to thank the Father for this experience."

He nodded. "I will, Cy. And I can assure you, I'll be talking to Him tonight, thanking Him for letting me share this safari with you."

The next morning, as Dr. P came in to meet me for breakfast, I could hear the smile in his voice before he even stepped through the door. He sat down, and before we ate, we bowed our heads and prayed.

About an hour after leaving camp, we picked up the tracks of a large male bongo. It wasn't long before we were successful in our pursuit—Dr. P had taken an exceptional bongo. As we celebrated with high-fives, the staff got to work skinning the animal. After taking numerous photos, Dr. P sat beside me in the forest, a grin so wide it seemed to shine.

As we prepared to leave the site, I grabbed Dr. P by the shirt and said, "Take a look around—make sure you're not leaving anything behind. Do you have your binoculars? Your camera? Your shell holder?" After a quick check, he nodded, "I'm ready."

On our way back, about fifteen minutes into our walk, we moved in a single-file line—our head tracker in the lead, followed by the PH, another tracker, then Dr. P, me, and a final tracker at the rear. Suddenly, Dr. P got caught in some vines and briars, completely stuck. I walked up with my pruning shears to help untangle him.

"Where are the shears I gave you?" I asked.

His face paled. "I think I left them where I shot the bongo."

"I'll send a tracker back to find them," I assured him.

Dr. P shook his head. "No way. He'll never find them in this jungle."

I just smiled. "Go hide and watch."

Even I had my doubts, but within ten minutes, the tracker jogged back, grinning like a Cheshire cat, holding Dr. P's pruning shears. We were both in shock.

Pygmy trackers are, without a doubt, the best in all of Africa. I've seen some skilled ones before, but nothing compares to them. In other parts of Sub-Saharan Africa, trackers work over dirt, sand, and even rocky terrain. But in the dense forest, these men track by reading the ground in ways most people can't even comprehend.

On my first day in the forest, I observed one of the head trackers closely. He walked at a steady pace, occasionally pointing to the ground. I saw nothing but leaves. Curious, I asked the PH what he was seeing. The PH bent down and lifted a large leaf, and beneath it, I could see a faint heat mark in the dirt where a foot had pressed into the ground. That's the kind of skill we were dealing with.

After reaching the Land Rover, we stopped for lunch. During some of our excursions, we'd hear loud thudding sounds coming from high in the trees—it was like someone was beating a drum. And then, without warning, a massive gorilla would appear, squatting just fifteen feet away. We were instructed to freeze and avoid eye contact. It happened at least once a day, and trust me, it would make you pucker up real quick if you know what I mean.

That afternoon, we tracked a group of dwarf buffalo. Within an hour, Dr. P had taken his second animal—a magnificent dwarf buffalo. To say he was a happy camper would be an understatement; You couldn't have wiped that grin off his face if you tried.

On days four and five, we focused on hunting duikers. If I recall correctly, Dr. P managed to get six out of the seven he was after.

Occasionally, while deep in the forest, we'd spot a Pygmy climbing high into a tree. Bees would be buzzing all around him as he reached into a hive. Moments later, he'd shimmy back down with a chunk of honeycomb, and we'd all share in the sweet, waxy treat.

Whenever we came across a small water hole or stream, it would be teeming with stunning butterflies—owl butterflies with beautifully patterned wings of all colors, many of them glowing in the dim light of the jungle.

I'll never forget the trip back to the airport. We had to drive through a rough part of Douala—not just rough roads, but rough sights. I sat in the middle seat with a PH on either side of me. I won't go into details, but even Dr. P, a man who had spent most of his career practicing medicine in life-and-death situations, stared straight ahead, visibly disturbed by what we saw.

In closing, I want to say that Dr. P is an exceptional man, and I truly believe that our journey into the jungles of Central Africa left a lasting impact on his life.

I still follow Dr. P online, and he and his wife continue to dedicate large sums of their own money to building schools, churches, water systems, and clinics in some of the most desperate parts of Africa. Kudos to them—I love them both, and I know my father would be incredibly proud of them.

A Side Note About the Bugs

Two years after returning home, I woke up one morning, getting ready for work, when I felt like I had an eyelash stuck in my eye. I walked into Olivia's office and asked her to check. She told me to bend over so she could take a closer look. After a few moments, she calmly said, "You have a worm in your eye."

I was in complete disbelief. "No way."

Our receptionist, who had overheard the conversation, quickly chimed in. "Cy, there's a good optometrist just two blocks from here. She's a friend—I'll give her a call."

When I arrived at the optometrist's office, a Black lady from South Africa walked up to me and asked, "Are you Cy?"

I nodded, and she led me to an exam chair. After a brief examination, she stepped back and gasped, "Oh my God! You have a worm in your eye."

She continued, "This is above my pay grade, but I know two specialists in downtown Austin. I'll call them now." Moments later, she returned and said, "They're expecting you—head over there right away."

I jumped into my car and drove 20 minutes through Austin traffic in the sweltering July heat. And let me tell you—after having a light shined on it, that worm started doing the Chubby Checker Twist inside my eye.

Upon arriving at the specialist's office, one of the two doctors was already waiting for me. On the way there, I had called Dr. P to explain the situation. He immediately told me, "In my medical studies, I took courses in tropical diseases. Tell the doctors to look up 'filarial worms.'"

The specialist examined my eye with a scope and light, then looked up and said, "Yep, you've got a worm in your eye."

I sighed. "You're the third person to tell me that today."

A second doctor walked in, examined me, and said, "Well, what do you want us to do?" (I'm not kidding.)

I stared at them. "I want You to get this damn worm out of my eye!"

They told me they could have a surgical room ready in about an hour. I agreed.

A nurse soon entered with a consent form and asked, "Would you mind if we film this? We need your permission."

"Sure, why not?" I said.

About 45 minutes later, they led me to a small surgical room packed with at least a dozen medical professionals. The doctor performing the procedure told me, "I'm going to put some drops in your eye—it's like liquid cocaine. You won't feel a thing."

A few moments after the drops took effect, he made a tiny incision in the outer layer of my eye and carefully extracted a worm—about 2 ¼ inches long and as thick as a small pencil lead. He placed it on a tray, and the nurse asked, "Doctor, what solution should I put it in for the lab?"

Without missing a beat, the doctor said, "Hell, I'd put it in some tequila."

The whole room burst into laughter.

The next morning, the doctors confirmed the diagnosis: filarial worm. I had to wait five days for the medication to arrive from India. It came in pill form, and I had to take several doses a day for 30 days. It was brutal—I felt like I had the flu nonstop for a month.

During my treatment, my wife Olivia and I attended a few social events. By then, my story had made its way onto YouTube, and people kept asking Olivia if she had noticed any symptoms before the worm appeared. Olivia, always the comedian, would joke, "Well, sometimes I caught him dragging his ass on the carpet." (Not true, but it always got a good laugh.)

A Final Note on Africa

Before I wrap up this story, I want to emphasize that I don't want to discourage anyone from visiting Africa. In my opinion, it is the number one destination in the world for big game hunting and adventure.

Over the past 45 years, I've been to the continent 40 times, visiting nine different countries, and this was the only time I ever had an issue.

So, if you're considering a trip to Africa—whether for hunting or sightseeing—I highly encourage you to go.

The Business of the Acquisition of Life

Keep reading—there are plenty more exciting adventures to come! I know I've sure enjoyed them.

Chapter 9
The African Princess

Folks, this chapter I'm about to write is going to be extremely difficult, and I'm going to handle it very delicately.

It's about a personal assistant—a Young lady I fell deeply in love with.

In about my fifth year with Cabela's, the assistant I had worked with for five years came to me one weekend and told me she was going to leave. It was like losing a sister I dearly loved.

She said, "Cy, I have to tell you—I need to quit."

Startled, I asked, "Why?"

With her lips quivering, she replied, "I can't spend another day in that office with the General Manager."

I said, "I understand. But don't quit Cabela's—it's a great company, and you've already got 10 years vested. Let me see if I can get You a job working for Dick and Mary."

That next week, Dick and Mary gladly hired her.

After she announced her departure, I began interviewing for a new assistant. Some of the other consultants were okay with someone who could type, use a computer, take notes, and talk well on the phone. Not me. I wanted someone who had a love and passion for our industry. I believed we owed our clients more. For some of them, we were preparing their dream destination—and I remembered what my first trip to Zambia, Africa, did for me.

That trip changed everything. It's why I left the Club Manager Business. I had a great and rewarding job, but it wasn't the passion God had planted in my heart at a very young age.

About two weeks into my search, a Young consultant I was mentoring walked into my office.

He said, "I know this Young girl down in Texas—she's guiding clients on the Triple 777, a famous exotic game ranch."

I said, "Give me her name and number. I'll give her a call."

That night, I called Olivia—Livy, as she was known. I introduced myself and started talking to her about the possibility of joining Cabela's as my assistant.

She was polite, but I felt a cold response. Still, in that one-hour conversation, I knew she was the one—and I knew it was my Father who had pointed me toward her.

A few days later, we spoke again—this time for about two hours. She was warming up, not quite there yet, but I could sense the shift.

Each time we talked, I became more convinced she was the one. Eventually, I said to her, "If you give me this chance, I promise—I'll make sure you earn a PhD in this industry."

She called me the next day and said, "I'll take your offer."

I asked, "How soon can you get here?"

She said, "Give me 30 days."

The day she arrived, two of my best friends were visiting for the Fourth of July. My home sat on a ridge overlooking Sidney, and from the paved road, there was a long gravel driveway—about 200 yards—with a winding turn that led up to the house. That part of western Nebraska is so flat that if your dog ran away, you could watch him running for miles.

At around 2:00 PM, Steve and Sara—my close friends—and I were enjoying some refreshing drinks when we saw a big white Dodge pickup pulling a cattle trailer packed to the brim.

Steve said, "Who is that?"

I replied, "I have no clue."

The truck pulled up and parked just below the deck. Out stepped what looked like Ellie May from The Beverly Hillbillies.

The first thing Steve did was elbow me in the ribs and say, "You sly dog."

I said, "Steve, seriously—I hired her sight unseen."

It was Miss Olivia.

She came up, introduced herself, and joined us for drinks. I caught Steve's wife, Sara, giving Olivia the side-eye—and she'd just met her! The old saying comes to mind: There can only be one queen in the hive.

The next morning, Steve and I took Olivia to her apartment. HR had arranged temporary housing until she could get settled.

As we were unloading the truck, Olivia jumped in the back, grabbed an oversized armchair, and handed it to Steve and me. She probably weighed no more than 110 pounds, soaking wet. As we took the chair from her, Steve and I locked eyes, both thinking the same thing: Can we even handle this chair ourselves?

We finally got it down, and all three of us sat on the grass and laughed.

The next day, we got Livy squared away at the office after she finished with HR. There were probably about seven women working there—travel agents, secretaries, and the like. You should've seen the looks they gave her—like sour buttermilk.

But over time, they warmed up to Olivia and learned to respect her. I already knew the world of good she was going to bring.

It was a different story with most of the men in the corporate office—about 300 of them. They followed Olivia around the building like a pack of beagles on a hot rabbit trail.

Olivia (Livy) settled in quickly, but she wanted to do everything, everything with me. At the time, I was playing a lot of Racket Ball, and she was eager for me to teach her. On many weekends, I'd head out to a ranch to practice shooting prairie dogs about an hour northeast of Sidney, and she always wanted to come along. She was at the house often, joining me for dinner. Some of the guys were calling her, trying to take her out, but she kept turning them down. It started to weigh heavily on me.

About four months in, I called her and said, "We need to have a talk."

As soon as she came up the stairs, the first words out of her mouth were, "Are you mad at me?"

I said, "No. Have a seat."

She sat down, and I said, "You're doing much better than I expected—and I expect perfection. But Olivia, you're 21 years old, and I'm 40."

She asked, "Am I not mature enough for you?"

"There's a big difference between 21 and 40," I said. "You are very mature, but still a Young woman. I'm becoming very attached to you, and we can't let that happen. Whether you like it or not, the hunting side of what we do is predominantly a man's world. You're very well aware of that."

She nodded in agreement.

We continued on the journey, and a year later, I asked her to marry me. She said, "I've wanted this for a long time."

Five months later, we got married at the Bellagio in Las Vegas. Originally, we'd hoped to marry in Tanzania, but Olivia's parents had been divorced for a while, and that plan didn't come together.

The weekend of our wedding in Vegas, we had numerous friends and family show up.

The morning of our wedding day, the hotel staff arranged a limo and driver to take us to get our marriage paperwork signed and stamped. On the way to the courthouse, the driver suddenly pulled over, rolled up the partition window, and looked at us in the rearview mirror with a serious expression.

"Who are you people?" he asked.

I laughed and said, "What do you mean?"

He replied, "Guys, this isn't my first rodeo. I've taken plenty of couples to get their marriage licenses, but I've never seen a guest list of 124 people for a Vegas wedding. I've been doing this for over seven years. Seriously—who are You?"

I said, "I'm Cy, and this is Olivia. We're just a couple in love."

He gave us a long look, then put the limo back in gear and drove us to the courthouse.

We got everything signed and stamped and headed back to the hotel. As we were getting out of the limo, I handed him a generous tip. He shook my hand and said, "I still don't believe you. You're both great storytellers."

Two hours later, I was in my tux and Olivia was in her gown. We walked through the casino to the Aria Ballroom, which was filled with flowers and plants. By the time we got on stage for the photographer to start taking pictures, there must have been a crowd of 300 people, being conservative. You'd have thought we were DJT and Melania.

Out of nowhere, a drunk man came running out of the crowd, yelling, "I love you!" I had to fend him off before the security guards carried him away, chewing him out the whole time.

In 30 minutes, we were husband and wife, and the celebration began—it was a huge party. For the next week, Livy and I visited several cities and rode every roller coaster we could find.

A week after we got back, Livy went on a 21-day safari with her dad, Dr. Pete. They were in Tanzania when 9/11 happened.

When Livy finally returned home, I had to reassign her to work under Dick and Mary—company policy prohibited her from working directly for me. We'd only been married a month when she called and asked me to go to lunch with her.

As we sat down, she looked at me and said, "Cy, what would you think if I ran for Mrs. Nebraska?"

I raised an eyebrow and asked, "Why?"

She said, "In this company, we all know what we know about conservation and outdoor adventures. But it's like trying to evangelize in a church. If I got lucky and won, I'd have a platform to share and educate outsiders."

I told her, "If that's your why, I'll support you 100%."

This was on a Monday. Then she said, "Great—I'm in the contest next Saturday. It's on the other side of the state."

My wheels started turning. I'd just promised my new wife I would support her 100%. I called a good friend who owned a ranch halfway between Sidney and the contest location, just south of Lincoln.

That Friday, Livy and I left work early and arrived at Jay's ranch around 5:00 PM. The day before, Livy had gotten her hair, nails, and toes done. She wore a cute sundress when we pulled up, and Jay and two cowboys came riding in—they'd been working cattle all day.

They dismounted, but the two cowboys were so timid— Livy's beauty had them too shy to look in her direction, like they feared a headlock if they stared too long.

The five of us—Livy, me, and the two cowboys—sat on a bench in the shade of an old barn. Jay jumped in the back of his truck, opened the ice chest, and asked if we wanted a cold beer. We all accepted, and he tossed each of us one. The cowboy at the far end pulled out a can of Copenhagen, packed it, and put a pinch in his lip. Livy asked him if she could share a dip. I thought those cowboys were going to faint—and Jay nearly fell out of the truck laughing.

We drank our beers, had dinner, and went to bed early.

The next morning, we had breakfast with the cowboys and headed to Lincoln for the contest. The event went late into the night, and Livy was crowned Miss Nebraska. It was early May.

We drove back to Jay's that night, stayed over, and headed home on Sunday. On the drive back, Livy informed me the Miss America pageant would be held in Hawaii in

June. She said she had to be there for three weeks and asked if I could come.

I told her there was no way I could leave for three weeks, but I had an outfitter in Hawaii I used for clients. I offered to visit him and spend the last three days with her in Honolulu—that way, I could expense my travel. Those three days were incredible. Livy didn't win, but it was an unforgettable adventure.

Here's where I'll fast-forward and bring this chapter to a close.

Livy and I spent ten great years together, traveling the world and sharing adventures. But it came to an end when she decided she wanted a baby.

Ten years earlier, just after we were married, she had asked me to get a vasectomy. I said, "I'll be glad to—but are you sure? Because when Mother Nature calls you to have a child—and she will—I won't be getting it reversed. So you'd better be absolutely sure."

She assured me she wanted to spend those years building her career and exploring life with me. I agreed. I was older, more mature—wiser, or so I thought.

Livy and I divorced amicably. We've remained distant friends.

If you remember, I told her that if she gave me one year, I'd give her a PhD in the business she loved. I kept that promise.

As a female consultant, Livy has since won every major hunting award in the world—except the Weatherby. That one's mostly awarded to men, though a few women have achieved that pinnacle.

I wish Livy all the best and truly believe her time will come.

I kept my promise.

Chapter 10
Cabelas Dick & Mary

I think it's a good time to share with my readers how Dick and Mary started Cabela's. In 1961, Dick was working for his father and the family lived in Chappell, NE. Dick's father ran a small furniture company in Chappell. Dick bought $45 worth of fishing flies and when he got home, he decided he'd try and sell them through an outdoor magazine.

As it was told, the story goes that the post was a small ad in the magazine that said "10 flies for $1," and they didn't get much activity. So later they put up another ad that said "10 flies free" and a fee of $10 for shipping and handling.

Keep in mind that this story was given to me while in Sidney by longtime friends over the years. Everyone agrees they started making a list of names, addresses, and phone numbers. As the list grew, it is my understanding that they started adding outdoor items to their list of clients. It's my understanding that it grew so fast that soon they had to rent the old Sears building in Sidney, NE, as the orders rolled in.

They grew very fast.

At some point, Dick asked his brother Jim if he would come. I understand he had an accounting degree from college and gladly accepted the offer. Shortly after, Frank and Jim started a catalog, and the company really took off.

Dick and Mary started building and remodeling their Sidney home and were adding on a 20,000 sq. foot game room. This took 3 years and was absolutely incredible.

I can remember many evenings going over to Dick and Mary's, sitting at their bar on the second floor, and discussing a multitude of subjects. Cabela's started a very aggressive building strategy all over the country. It seemed like they were putting up at least one store location in America every year. It was a very fast spurt of growth.

I continued to find new destinations for our valued clients, but the pace had slowed down tremendously, and I was spending more time in the office.

As the years passed, my exposure to the outdoor world advanced tremendously. In 2004, we were all in a big meeting one morning — about 70 of us were informed we would probably go public, and they were preparing us for the changes.

Six months later, we made a public offering, and things changed dramatically. We went from a small family-run company of about 7,000 employees and went from the first Cabela's store in Sidney to about seven more states in numerous locations all over the US.

Shortly after we went public, Mary and I decided to go home to Texas and start the next life in the industry we loved. Lindsey and I moved to Dripping Springs just outside of Dripping Springs. Within the first year, I started a small consulting group with a consultant I had worked with for years, and soon we added a Young consultant. We had done wing-shooting out of Georgia while we were still consulting with Cabela's.

In my second year, Dick and Mary asked me to arrange an elephant hunt for each of them in Zimbabwe. I had been in a Fed meeting but had not met Mary yet. I remember in that second year, I was over visiting three countries in Africa — Botswana, Namibia, and Zimbabwe — whenever I was there. I had the staff come pick me up in Vic Falls on the trip to the camp in the Matetsi region. I asked my driver how Dick and Mary were doing with their hunting, and he informed me that Dick had shot a nice elephant — about 60 lbs per side — and he informed me Mary had just taken her elephant, shot her bull about the time of my arrival in Vic Falls. I asked the driver, "Instead of going to the camp, why don't we go see Dick and Mary in the field with her elephant harvest?"

When we came over a small ridge, I could see I had witnessed a scene I had viewed many times. I never personally wanted an elephant, but I have arranged many elephant hunts for numerous clients.

The scene looked like this: You see a couple of Land Rovers, a big elephant on its side, with at least 15 natives cutting the elephant up. Numerous tribal members show up, taking pieces of the elephant meat back to their village for the family.

Dick and Mary were in lounge chairs with an ice-down ice chest loaded with Dom P. Champagne. I walked up, shook Dick's hand. Mary got up to give me a hug, caught her sari pants on her lounge chair, and slipped down. As I was helping her up, she said, "Cy, I am so embarrassed to meet you for the first time." I assured her to relax. "You should be in a celebration when we shoot…"

To wind this story down, it is fond memories of Dick and Mary. We lost Dick Cabela on March 4th, 2016. Dick Cabela was 77 years old. And we lost Mary on May 30th, 2023. She was 84 years old. I still have very fond memories of both of them. I can say without a doubt that they were two of the kindest individuals I have ever worked with in my 45 years of consulting. They worked very hard to grow the largest outdoor hunting company in the world. Bar none — everyone that was ever in their presence, they treated like family.

Speaking, Dick and Mary had 9 children and kept in close touch with all of them until the days they passed. The Cabela's eldest "D" has followed in their parents' footsteps and has started a foundation supporting the conservation and protection of wildlife all over the world.

You guessed it — Chris Kyle. I mentioned in an earlier chapter how, at one juncture in my consulting career, I was raising money for our warriors by doing top-end auctions at the conventions at SCI and DSC, the largest conventions in the world for hunting.

I think it was 2008 when I arranged my first auction for SCI. It was in Vegas that year. In the consulting business, it is imperative to make those two shows annually if you're serious. When I first called SCI to suggest doing this for an auction item, they said, "Ey, I don't know if this will work. You know, we do auctions for so many causes." I said, "Ma'am, if SCI doesn't want to work for our warriors, you don't need me as a booth buyer to be on your floor." I had her patch me to the President of SCI at that time, and he accepted it immediately.

While I was visiting with Chris, a Dallasite came up, barged in between us, and interrupted Chris and me. The man started with, "So you're the badass Chris Kyle?" Chris very politely said, "I'm an American Soldier (Navy Seal) fighting for our country." The guy popped off again, and Chris, in a flash, grabbed him from the back, picked him up, gave him one of those squeezes that instantly knocked you out for a few seconds, and laid him down softly on the ground. He woke up in a few seconds, grabbed his gear, and walked off without a word. If you have never seen it done, it's amazing.

Chapter 11
The American Sniper

You guessed it—Chris Kyle. I mentioned in an earlier chapter how, at one juncture in my consulting career, I was raising money for our warriors by doing top-end auctions. These took place at conventions like SCI and DSC—the largest hunting conventions in the world.

In, I think, 2008, I arranged my first auction for SCI. It was in Las Vegas that year. In the consulting business, it is imperative to make those two shows annually—IF You're serious.

When I first called SCI to suggest doing this for an auction item, the lady said, "I don't know if this will work. You know, we do auctions for so many causes." I said, "Ma'am, if SCI doesn't want to work for our warriors, you don't need me as a booth buyer to be on your floor." She patched me through to the President of SCI at the time, and he accepted it immediately.

That first military auction ever done in Vegas that year was an overwhelming success. The auction was built around Marcus Luttrell. You'll probably remember Marcus from his book and the movie Lone Survivor. The buyer of the auction would get to hunt with Marcus on a large ranch in South Texas for a trophy whitetail deer.

The retail value of that hunt was $5,400. That Saturday night auction item was number one on the list. We were expecting Marcus to attend, but at the last minute, he had to have back surgery and couldn't make it.

The Young lady who had worked post-op after Marcus returned from his issues in the Middle East—Lt. Colonel S.H.—arranged for Chad Fleming to fill in for Marcus. Chad was one tough warrior himself. He had fought in many of his own battles.

It was my first time in Vegas to work with Chad. To my recollection, Chad was Special Forces and on his second tour of duty, lost the lower part of his left leg and had it replaced with a prosthetic. A year later, he was such a badass that our military allowed him to return to active duty. That's extremely rare. If I'm not mistaken, Chad had earned three Silver Stars. (Amazing.) He was elite—of the elites.

That Saturday night, the main auction room was packed. Men in tuxedos and women in gowns with expensive jewelry. Chad got up on stage to kick it off with the auctioneer and knocked it out of the park. He had the crowd in his hands.

Things started to slow down at around $27,000. Chad came back out, and the crowd went wild. Before we knew it, the bid amount had reached $70,000. The auctioneer hit the gavel. But then he paused and said, "Wait a minute."

He came back on and said, "Folks, the man who just bought the hunt has informed us he has a friend who wants to tag along—not to hunt, just to go. He's offering another $70,000."

That $5,400 deer hunt went for $140,000. The crowd went crazy. People were dancing on tables. That's the kind of patriotism that attendees live and breathe in long hunting. My staff and I were treated like royalty.

Back to Chris Kyle, the main part of the story, but I needed you to follow the full arc. The summer after the Vegas event, I took a trip to Dallas to meet with a gentleman on the DSC board. He asked me if we could do an auction like that with DSC.

I said, "Yes, sir, we can, but I have a few stipulations." He said, "Fire away." I said, "Of the total amount raised, I want 50% going to the soldiers, and I want a booth free of charge for the soldiers so people can come in and meet these men." His reply: "Absolutely."

Two years later, we arranged another auction with Chris Kyle for the main event. The year before the big one with Chris and DSC, I was at a major event for Marcus Luttrell. I heard big rifles sounding off on the back deck of Rough Creek Lodge. Two big cowboys were shooting long-range rifles. You could tell by their positions—these guys were pros. That's when I first met Chris.

As the shots rang out, you'd hear the ping of metal as they struck their targets. Chris and I chatted briefly. Later, I asked if he'd be willing to let me use him in an auction hunt at DSC in, I think, 2008. He agreed.

Over the next year and a half, we'd periodically catch up. That summer, before the event, I met with the Young lady who had started the Boot Campaign. She asked if we could host an auction as a big event. She had set it up at a private gun club in Dallas. I was unsure if we'd raise what we needed, but I agreed.

On the day of the event, I arrived at midday. The guys were shooting sporting clays. I grabbed a golf cart and found Chris. It was good to see him again.

While I was visiting with Chris, a Dallasite came up, barged in, and interrupted us. The man said, "So you're the badass Chris Kyle." Chris politely responded, "I'm an American soldier—Navy SEAL—fighting for our country."

The guy popped off again. In a flash, Chris grabbed him from behind, gave him one of those three squeezes that knocked you out, laid him gently on the ground, and then walked away silently. The guy stood up, dazed, and left. It was amazing.

After lunch, we had the auction. Chris was on stage with me as I prepared it. It got started. At one point, bidding slowed at $7,000. I took the mic, tried to stir the crowd, and got it up to $11,000. Then I said, "We're pulling it."

I hugged Chris and told him we'd try again. That wouldn't be our first DSC auction and fail. Chris smiled, and we had cocktails in the shade. I'd been offered a plains game hunt on a private ranch in Zimbabwe. It was on the border of Zimbabwe and South Africa, near Beitbridge. It was for a couple—2 men, 2 women.

Didn't matter. Besides hunting plains game, the couple would be with Chris Kyle and get instructions on long-distance shooting. (Sniper work.)

That Saturday night, Chris was in the booth with me and the staff. Around 1 a.m., after breakfast with the DSC group, Chris and his team showed up. One of my partners noticed a man in a hoodie nearby and got worried.

"Do you think Chris sees him?" he asked. I said, "He sees everything." Chris calmly reached inside his sweatshirt and pulled a pistol—then revealed it was an old man sleeping! I almost fell down laughing.

Later, during breakfast, I asked Chris how he was doing with PTSD. He said he was doing fine, but the one thing that drove him crazy was all the people complaining about minor inconveniences. "They don't know what a f***ing problem is."

Soon after, I went upstairs to get ready for an event. Within ten minutes, my team called. There was an issue. I returned, fixed it, and Chris and I headed to one of the ballroom events.

These were black-tie affairs. Chris showed up in fatigues. I had at least worn a sports coat. A man in a tux stopped us and told Chris he was underdressed. Chris said, "Didn't have time. I'm the keynote."

We sat with Marcus Luttrell and others. A female enlisted Army member told a story about Jessica Lynch. Chris turned red. "I was there," he said. "Looking for my brother." He gave her a look. "You weren't there." Then he walked out. She followed.

Minutes later, Chris returned and showed me a piece of paper with her name and number. I said, "Throw it away."

When we were called up, I told Chris to stay seated. He refused. We went up. I handed the mic to the auctioneer, but Chris took it.

In a cowboy voice, he said, "I'm so excited I can't stand it. I've never hunted animals in Africa." The crowd roared. Then he said, "Unless you voted for Obama, you're not going!" The place erupted.

The auction was a success. Two men behind me bought it. I knew them. Two months later, I got a call—Chris and Chad Littlefield were both dead. Shot.

A week later, we were at Chris Kyle's memorial in Cowboys Stadium. 10,000 people. Not a dry eye.

One of the original buyers backed out. He said, "Keep my money for the warriors." The other called and asked if he could find a replacement soldier. I said, "Good luck replacing Chris Kyle."

A week later, he called again. Jeff Kyle, Chris's brother, wanted to honor Chris. And he did.

In honor of Chris Kyle and in memory of him and Chad Littlefield—his best friend, who died with him—RIP, my friends.

In closing, when Chris was overseas, the enemy had nicknames for him:

• Devil of Ramadi

• Ninja Smoke

• Tex, the Legend

Chapter 12
Mexico Pigskin

On one of my wing-shooting trips—back when I still had business with Cabela's and before things got too dangerous with the cartels—I visited a wing-shooting lodge in Mexico. It was called Don Quixote Lodge, located in San Fernando. We would usually cross the Texas-Mexico border near Reynosa.

The area was a wing shooter's paradise. Depending on your timing, you could hunt dove, quail, ducks, and geese—sometimes all in the same adventure. As I recall, it was early December when I arrived.

On my first day, I joined a fairly large group of hunters. Among them were two familiar faces—NFL legends Leroy Jordan and Bob Lilly. I had met Bob before, but this was my first time meeting Leroy. Both were stars for the Dallas Cowboys back in the late '60s and early '70s.

That night at dinner, DT—an old friend of mine and the lodge owner—asked if I'd go out quail hunting the next day with Leroy and a couple of oil field guys. I gladly agreed.

The following morning, after breakfast, we loaded into a van and headed to a large Estancia about an hour away. I remember the air was chilly, and the ranch itself was massive. We spent the day walking and flushing coveys, only stopping for a quick lunch. The wind made things tough, and the quail didn't make it easy either. But by late afternoon, the four of us had shot an unbelievable number of birds.

As we climbed back into the van, I could see Leroy was stiff and sore—he was in his late 60s at the time. And needless to say, football is a brutal sport. Leroy had been an All-American at Alabama and was drafted early by the Cowboys. He played either as a defensive end or linebacker—maybe even a middle linebacker. While he wasn't big by pro football standards—just over six feet and somewhere in the low 200s—he more than made up for it with his instincts and ability to get to the ball.

I heard Leroy groan as he got in the van. On the ride back to the lodge, I told him, "You better grab some muscle relaxers and join me in the hot tub. I'm having the staff bring me a big, strong cactus drink." He grinned and said, "Count me in."

At dinner that evening, I asked Leroy what he wanted to hunt the next day. "I'd like to hunt with you if that's okay," he said. "Of course," I told him. "Let's hit the laguna and go after some ducks." His face lit up. "That was my favorite growing up." I smiled and said, "Leroy, I'm gonna give you the best hunt of your life." He laughed and said, "I've been on some good ones."

We got up early the next morning and made a short drive to the beach where a blow-through laguna waited. On the ride in, I laid out the plan: "We each have a license, and the guide has one too. That's 20 ducks each—60 total. Let's go get 'em." Leroy's eyes lit up like a kid on Christmas morning.

We were dropped off along the shoreline. The bird boys started putting out decoys while Leroy and I set up. The ducks began flooding in, cupping their wings and landing near the boys as they worked. I turned to Leroy and said, "You shoot 'til you're tired. I'm only pulling the trigger if one's wounded and trying to get away."

For nearly two hours, Leroy fired nonstop. I think he came pretty close to hitting the limit. On the way back to camp, he leaned over and said, "Man, I wish my buddies back in Alabama could see this. They'd never believe it."

That evening over dinner, Leroy asked if we could hunt again the next day. I told him I'd love to, but I had business to handle with the lodge owner. "I'll have dinner with y'all tomorrow night," I said. "Then I've got to travel down to Trevé Lodge on the lake. We're filming a duck hunting series there."

"I'll see you and Bob at dinner," I promised.

That night, after a few drinks, I pulled out an NFL football and asked Leroy and Bob to sign it for my nephew's Christmas gift. As they were autographing it, I asked Leroy who the toughest runner he ever had to tackle.

Without hesitation, he said, "Hands down—Larry Csonka. That guy was a load. Anytime I saw him break through the line, I just wanted to head back to the bench and tell the coach to mail me my last check. You can stick a fork in me—I'm done."

The next day, I got shuttled down to Trevé. It was cold, wet, and miserable. I unloaded my gear, went to the bar, and ordered some nachos. I told them I'd go out the next morning.

About two hours later, in walked Larry Csonka. We knew of each other from working on hunting shows, so he came over and joined me at the table. He ordered nachos, and we mainly talked about how much of a pain-producing hunting show could be. Then we got into football and ranching.

Later that evening, Larry said he was bushed and planned to get up early to fish. I mentioned I had brought another football with me and asked if he'd mind signing it for my nephew. "Let's do it now," he said.

Turned out we were staying in rooms right next to each other. I ran to grab the ball and knocked on his door. He invited me in, wearing nothing but jogging shorts—and I swear, I thought I was staring at a lowland gorilla I'd seen once in Equatorial Africa.

He sat on the edge of the bed, rolling the football in his massive hands, fingers sticking in all directions. When he noticed Bob and Leroy's signatures, he laughed and said, "These guys are all in the Hall of Fame, and I hunted with both of them at that camp before I got here!"

Then he added, "You know, Bob Lilly could hit harder than a junkyard dog. I don't think any linebacker ever hit me that hard." We spent a while reminiscing about the game before I called it a night.

The next morning, I got up to meet Larry for breakfast, but it was raining hard, pouring like cats and dogs. If memory serves me right, we didn't go out that day.

That hunt became one of many unforgettable experiences I've had with celebrities. Over the years, I've hunted with pro athletes, congressmen, senators, and some of our nation's elite warriors. I can truly say I've been blessed. I'm convinced it was all part of my Father's plan.

Side note—there was a time I spent three days with General "Stormin' Norman" Schwarzkopf, shortly after he returned from Desert Storm. We built a great friendship, and I was helping him plan a trip to Guatemala, to one of the finest sailfish fisheries in the world. Sadly, he was diagnosed with prostate cancer and never got to go.

He was truly an incredible man.

Chapter 13
The Yankee Goes to Iceland

I'm not the Yank, but a close friend of mine who started out as a client 25 years ago called me and said,

"Can you book us on a goose/reindeer hunt in Iceland?"

I replied,

"If I can't, nobody can."

Big (R) was one of those men you could just look at and know you would never want to get in a dust-up with — you would likely come out on the short side. But once I got to know him, he was a teddy bear. Behind the rugged veneer, he had a heart of gold.

With his last name, I just knew he had to be part of true traffic. After a few years and trips together, I got up the nerve to ask him, but his answer wasn't yes, and it wasn't no.

Big (R) was born and raised in New York and had a big company in Manhattan. I can't say what he did because I don't want to give away his cover — if he was a Mob Boss. Big (R) gives me a call one day and says,

"The crew and I want to go hunt in Iceland."

I asked him what size group he could muster up, and his reply was 8–10. So I booked it 8 months out — for me and a group of 8.

Well, time passed, and a month out, Big (R) was having no luck filling the group!

Fortunately, I always keep an Ace in my deck. I had good luck calling some friends (clients) and saying in August —

"I'm going — if we can gather 3 or 4 friends, join us."

At the last minute, I found a group of 4 who wanted to go up for the goose-hunting portion. So now we had a group of 8 — Big (R), his wife, his young son, and 4 Texans.

A month later, we all met up in New York and took a flight to Reykjavik, Iceland's capital and largest city.

We arrived early afternoon. The drivers picked us up and we were off to Reykjavik. It was about an hour's drive.

Halfway there, the drivers pulled into a location similar to a ski resort — but instead, it was a very large white mud lake with steam rising from it. There were large groups of people taking a lazy hot mud bath.

We parked, went in, and rented gear to take a mud bath with about 200 people. The mud lake was so big, there was no congestion. We hadn't been in the pool very long when Big (R) floated over to me and said,

"This is great — we're in Iceland, home of some of the hottest women in the Northern Hemisphere, and taking a hot mud bath."

We floated around for about an hour, then changed into our clothes and headed to our hotel. We all met in the lobby around 6:00 p.m. and walked down to a restaurant about 3 blocks away.

Our guide said it was the best restaurant in town.

On a U.S. scale (1–10), it was about a 7.

As soon as we opened our menus, we were caught off guard — the items listed were pan-fried seal, horse steak, and whale blubber sautéed in pork slime.

This was about 17 years ago, and the average cost of a plate of food was about $200 US dollars — a little pricey. We all enjoyed our meal, and afterward, a lady at the table wanted a Brandy Alexander. We were in no hurry, so she ordered her drink.

The Brandy Alexander was $56 US.

The next day, we all got up and went downstairs for breakfast, about $30 a pop.

On the third and last day, we said goodbye to our Texans, and we headed south to our reindeer location. They call them reindeer in Iceland.

When we got to our hotel in Southeast Iceland, we put our gear in our rooms and went to the hotel dining room. We all ordered reindeer — and it was excellent. We were hunting in an area called Petitfoss Egilsstadir.

On the six-hour drive to the reindeer area, I was riding with our guide, and Big (R) and his family were following in a red soccer mom van with their driver.

During the drive, I started talking with our guide and asked him if he had ever hunted reindeer in this area.

He replied,

"I have never hunted reindeer — period."

It kind of took me back for a second, but I stayed cool. He was a nice young lad in his early to mid-20s. I calmly said,

"How is this going to work?"

He informed me the area was very large and that each game manager was in charge of the hunts — you can't hunt without him. It's Icelandic law.

Early the next morning, we drove to meet the hunt manager. He couldn't speak a word of English. I still kept my cool. We said we needed to pre-shoot our rifles to make sure they were zeroed. I told our driver/guide, who explained it to the hunt manager in their native tongue.

The old, weathered man went into his house, grabbed an old cereal box that was light blue and green, and put a green circle in the middle of the box.

"You and Big (R) are going to pick out the bulls you want to harvest. We will count to three, and you both shoot."

I looked at my number two guide and said, "That dog isn't going to hunt."

(Slang for: "That's not going to happen.")

I asked both guides to hold back — I would take it from here. Big (R) and I got into position, lying on the ground. I made sure Big (R) knew which bull I wanted him to shoot.

The bull was bedded down.

I told Big (R), "When that bull stands up, let it fly. Remember, slow, gentle squeeze."

It seemed like forever, but when the bull started to stand up, Big (R) let it rip — and the bull collapsed right where he stood. We approached the downed bull. The guides were hollering like they had never seen this before. Guide 1 and Guide 2 were talking in their native tongue. I asked Guide 1, "What are y'all discussing?"

In English, he said, "One — he had never seen a reindeer shot at that position."

Guide 2 said, "I have a tag — will you help me get that second good bull?"

The excitement made him forget he was also guiding a client, but I agreed. We got back on the herd and Guide 1 dropped the second bull — a damn good bull, but nothing like Big (R)'s. It was now lunchtime, so we loaded the reindeer and had lunch.

After lunch, we found another herd, and I took my bull. Here is where it gets funny: We drove to the packer plant to deliver our bulls. It was a government-run station for harvested reindeer — there must have been 30 bulls hanging up.

Big (R) was still grinning from ear to ear. I asked one of the officials, "What do you think of my bull?" The official said Big (R) and I had timed the wrong time — we had accomplished trophy-wise success, but the officials only cared about weight value.

(A cultural difference.)

A couple of days later, we were heading back to New York with a very successful trip to Iceland. But the moral of the story is: When you know what you're doing, regardless of what country you're in, you have to take the reins.

But always remember:

(IT'S NOT ABOUT THE KILL.)

Chapter 14
Jaguars of Paraguay

Sometime in the early 2000s, I contacted a good friend of mine named Rocky McBride. Rocky grew up in Alpine, Texas, and played football for Texas Tech for a couple of years, but he's best known for being the Top Cat Man in the world. There's no other man alive who knows more about wild cats—not even a close second.

In earlier years, I used to send Rocky to my clients who wanted to hunt mountain lions. Whenever someone wanted to go after a lion, Rocky was my go-to guy.

Over the years, I got to know Rocky well. Being a McBride, he was different in the best kind of way—a man's man. He had a brother named Rowdy and a sister named Randy. They all grew up in West Texas, and all three were tougher than a bus station steak.

Rocky spent half his time in Alpine, hunting everything you can imagine in that region of West Texas. The other half, he devoted himself to his projects in Australia and South America, primarily researching and studying jaguars in the jungles of Paraguay.

One of Rocky's family's other ventures involved reestablishing pumas in Florida through a state-run wildlife program.

One day, I called Rocky and asked if I could come down to Paraguay and help him capture some jaguars.

Rocky simply said, "Come on down."

A week later, I was on a plane headed to Asunción, the capital of Paraguay, located near the Paraguay River at the confluence with the Pilcomayo. Paraguay is a landlocked, upper-middle-income country. Despite a strong economy, one in four people lives in poverty. The population is both Latino and Hispanic.

At that time, I had already spent some time in Argentina, Brazil, and a bit in Venezuela. Rocky and his partner owned a large ranch near Filadelfia in the northwest corner of Paraguay, in a region known as the Grand Chaco—a vast jungle that borders Bolivia.

Upon arrival in Asunción, I met up with Rocky, who picked me up in his little 150 Cessna airplane. We loaded my gear and headed to Filadelfia. If I remember right, the flight took about three and a half hours.

When we landed, Rocky explained that Filadelfia was primarily a Mennonite colony called Fernheim, founded in the early 1930s by about 1,700 evangelical Mennonite refugees. It was immediately obvious that they had a very tight-knit community.

After grabbing what we needed, we flew out to the ranch. When I say we were in the middle of nowhere, I mean it. We were greeted by Rocky's wife, Monica, and their son, Caleb. We had dinner, settled in for the night, and talked through the week's plans.

The next morning at daylight, we packed up the truck and the dogs. Rocky, Caleb, and I were ready to roll.

As Rocky loaded the dogs into the kennels at the back of the truck, he called them by name—Griz, One-Ear, Beaver Breath, and others. At first glance, they didn't look like much, but those dogs were some of the finest cat dogs in the world. Rocky had a bloodline of cat dogs second to none.

Caleb was probably about twelve years old at the time. I said, "Rocky, are you seriously going to leave him out here in the middle of the jungle?"

Rocky replied,

"He needs to learn his lesson—he knows how to get back."

It was close, but we didn't get any strikes that day. (For context: the dogs start barking wildly when they pick up the scent of a cat.)

Later that afternoon, as we were driving back, Rocky spotted a dwarf brocket deer. He handed me the shotgun and said,

"Go shoot that deer."

I took the shot, and as we were loading the deer into the truck, Rocky said,

"That's the biggest set of antlers I've ever seen on a brocket."

I thought he was joking. (We'll come back to that.)

The next day, we had two strikes. The first was a Geoffrey cat, the second an ocelot. When we reached the tree, Rocky was already on his toes, flashlight in hand, shining it into the hollow of a tree trunk.

I said, "Rocky, I want to get a picture."

He told me, "Stand back."

He reached his bare arm in, and just then, a brown armadillo shot out of the trunk. Rocky chuckled and said,

"400's gotta be fast."

They weren't large cats, but they made up for it with pure speed. We didn't spot a jaguar that day, but we had another brocket deer for supper—and it was excellent.

On day three, around 11:00 AM, we got a strike on a jaguar. Everything happened fast. Rocky shouted,

"Grab the dart gun and the drug box! I've got to catch up with the dogs."

I yelled back, "Rocky, should I bring water?" (Big mistake.)

As he sprinted off, Rocky called over his shoulder,

"We'll have that jaguar treed in 300 yards or less."

By the time I caught up, we were about two miles into the jungle. Rocky was lying under the tree with the dogs barking wildly above him. I collapsed next to him and looked up to see… it was a puma, not a jaguar.

Suddenly, something thumped against my chest. Rocky had tossed me a pistol.

"What's this for?" I asked.

"You need to shoot the puma," he said.

"The dogs won't leave until it hits the ground."

I didn't want to, but we had no choice. We had to get back to the truck—without water, we'd expire in the jungle.

We completed the task and started the long trek back.

Halfway back, I told Rocky,

"I'm so dehydrated, I don't think I can make it."

He said we were near a small watering hole beneath a tree—maybe 50 yards away. We knelt down to drink.

"Rocky, don't drink that just yet—"

He already had.

As I dipped my hat into the water, I noticed something beneath the surface.

"What's that?" I asked.

He looked and replied,

"Oh, that? That's a Tapir Turd. Don't worry about it."

We bounced our way back to the truck, loaded the dogs, drank more water, and headed back to the ranch house.

When we arrived, we could barely get out of the truck. I had never been that physically exhausted in my life. It felt like a near-death experience.

I left for the States the next day.

We didn't end up catching a jaguar, but I saw plenty of other wildlife that calls the jungles of Paraguay home.

Chapter 15
The Mozambique Emerald

Sometime in the early 2000s, I took an exploratory trip to Mozambique in search of affordable Cape Buffalo hunts.

At the time, Outdoor Adventures was sending loads of clients to South Africa for those short 7-day package hunts for the plains game. We were selling them like hotcakes. Around then, African clients began seriously looking for Cape Buffalo hunts, so I figured—if we could offer a quality 7-day Buffalo hunt at a good price, hunters could hop a short flight into Mozambique and back out just as easily.

I flew from Johannesburg, South Africa, to Beira, Mozambique. The country was just getting back into hunting after years of civil war, and the government was looking to bring in cash flow after a long dry spell.

So I hopped over to Beira and met up with an old friend and professional hunter I'd hunted with twice before in Zambia—Abie DuPloy.

Abie met me at the Beira airport and drove me to one of his beach hangouts along the shores of the Indian Ocean. It was a little touristy spot where clients often came for lunch. There were small palapas with thatched umbrella roofs, tables, and chairs. A really chill place to grab a couple of cold beers and some prawns with Pele-Pele sauce.

They had other seafood, but that was the locals' go-to dish.

Abie and I sat down around noon, ordered beer and prawns, and waited for some government officials to arrive. We were supposed to meet and pitch them on structuring a new Cape Buffalo hunt. They were scheduled to show up around 3 PM.

Not long after we sat down, I noticed a local guy sitting a couple of tables over, trying to get my attention. I figured he wanted to sell me something. I got Abie to call him over using their local dialect.

The man walked over slowly, hunched, carrying something hidden beneath a large cloth napkin. He sat next to me and pulled the napkin off the object. I nearly fainted.

It was a pure emerald crystal, about nine inches in diameter and eight and a half inches tall, embedded in a rock the size of a large coffee mug.

When I tell you it was stunning—I mean stunning.

I asked Abie to find out what he wanted for it. Abie said the man wanted $1,200 US dollars.

Folks—that was a steal.

I asked Abie if I could get it out of the country. He said, "Fifty-fifty chance."

I said, "What if I get caught?"

He replied, "Then you'll spend a few years in a Mozambique prison—with little chance of getting out alive—and plenty of black prisoners who'd love to have a pretty white girlfriend."

I turned it down under duress.

Just about then, the government officials showed up. We sat with them and chatted for a while. In the end, they agreed we could organize a Cape Buffalo hunt for $500 USD per hunter, including tags, permits, dipping, packing, and a four-day hunt. With Abie's fee added in, it was an all-in hunt for around $2,000 USD. Even back then, that was dirt cheap.

As the sun set, Abie and I went to his travel camper on the beach. We had to be up by 7:30 AM to catch a short charter flight into the hunting camp. I still couldn't stop thinking about that emerald.

That night in camp, I told Abie, "I could've bought that emerald. Taken it on the charter flight, cut it down, wrapped it, dried it with salt, and stuffed it inside a buffalo cape for shipment to the States."

On top of that, I was under the Cabela's umbrella—if anything went sideways, they could've gotten me out of trouble. Abie laughed and said, "You're not the first one tempted."

He told me about a guy from Miami who had just smuggled one out. It had a market value of over one million dollars in the States. Needless to say, I didn't sleep much that night.

The next morning, we got up and rounded up about eight local natives who carried all our gear on their heads into the swamps.

The swamp started just behind the camp. The plan was to wade through water and elephant grass until we found buffalo.

That first day, we were unsuccessful and ended up overnighting on a little island in the swamp. At dinner, Abie told me the guys didn't want to stay on that island because they believed it was haunted.

I asked, "Why do you think they think that?"

Abie laughed and said, "Notice anything? Since we got here, we haven't heard a single boooong." See, all those little swamp islands had baboons—but not this one. After dinner, we went to our tent and swapped old hunting stories. I told him a few from our Zambia days.

The next morning, we had breakfast and started tracking buffalo again. By noon, we found a massive herd. The trick to finding them was watching for large flocks of white egrets flying up and down through the tall grass. That's the giveaway. You get close, find the bull you're after, and get your shot.

By that point in my career, I had taken a few buffalo— but never in swamp country.

Abie and I slowly inched into the herd. You could hear the bulls breathing, flatulating, and sloshing through the water.

At one point, Abie parted some sawgrass and pointed to a bull's shoulder. We were so close that my .416 couldn't have been more than five feet from the animal. When I squeezed off the shot, all hell broke loose. The herd was much larger than we'd thought. All we could do was hit the ground, lie in the water, and cover our heads with sawgrass. When things finally calmed down, Abie and I checked ourselves—aside from a few cuts and bruises, we were still in one piece.

But it was a closer call than either of us wanted.

After we capped out the buffalo, we packed up and headed back to the base camp.

That night, we got a warning. A serious storm was blowing in. Abie said, "We've got to load up and get back to the landing strip." The staff had an old eight-wheeled Unimog, a leftover from the war days. We drove through the storm all night—and let me tell you, it got hairy.

To this day, I reckon serious prayer was the only reason we made it out alive.

The next day we cleaned up, chartered back to Beira, and I caught a night flight out to Johannesburg. I forgot to mention—my legs were shredded from that sawgrass. The first thing I did when we got back to Beira was hit a local pharmacy for antibiotics.

Two days later, I arrived in Sidney, Nebraska, beat up, bruised, and cut to hell. How I didn't catch a serious infection is still a mystery to me.

We accomplished what we set out to do, but it was one hell of a whirlwind. I've since returned to Mozambique for one more safari. It's now becoming a pretty stable hunting destination.

Chapter 16
Sailfishing PAR-Excellence Guatemala

I know by the title you think I'm going to jump into Sailfishing—and I will—but I first have to make a comparison with Dove Shooting. I know that sounds strange—the way my mind works.

I don't know how many of y'all have hunted Dove in Argentina, but most likely, the first time a dove hunter has hunted Dove in Argentina, those guys are going to tell you stories you're not going to believe. If you have ever hunted Doves in Mexico, a great Dove hunt in Mexico is an OFF day in Argentina. In Argentina, it's just how many Doves in a day do you want to hunt? 200 birds, 300 birds, 1000 birds a day or more—you just shoot until you're out of shells or out of energy.

Well, Sailfishing in Guatemala is like Dove hunting in Argentina.

The key is being in Guatemala in late January through the 1st of April. Strap in tight because you're in for a fight. At that time of year, the Sailfish are in close, so you don't have to travel out into the ocean.

I was at Cabela's and doing my R&D on Guatemala and Sailfishing, and I couldn't believe what I was hearing. So, I decided to fly down there in March. I took a flight down to Guatemala City, the country's capital. My team picked me up and drove me to Puerto San Jose and the surrounding area of Iztapa—it's known as the Sailfishing Capital of the World! I had caught Sailfish before in other fisheries around the world, but you may catch two or three on a good day.

We arrived at the lodge the first afternoon, and I settled into a very nice lodge overlooking the ocean. I went mid-week and had the lodge to myself. Before going down, I'd called my girlfriend in Houston and asked her to fly down and fish a couple of days with me.

The first day, Randy hadn't made it down yet, so I just went by myself with the crew. That first morning, we boarded the boat and hadn't gone out 20 minutes when they dropped the baited lines and teasers—we had our first Sailfish on in 10 minutes. And it was one after another, sometimes two at a time. We stopped to boost at 2 in the afternoon, and by that time, I had brought 26 Sails to the boat and released (read that again). And these were the big Pacific Sails that averaged 100 lbs.

Randy made it in that night for dinner, and I decided the next day we would chill out and get caught up. We hadn't seen each other, and to be honest, I needed some rest after that first day of fishing.

On my first day at the lodge, I didn't see a soul—not even the pool boy. At 10:00 a.m., it was already bright and sunny, so I suggested to Randy, "Let's go sit by the pool", and she agreed. She came out about 10 minutes after me in a skinny red bikini, and within 20 minutes, Guatama men were everywhere trimming bushes, climbing palm trees, and pruning palms. It was starting to rattle Randy, so we went back into the room after about 30 minutes by the pool. That evening, we had an early dinner and retired to our room.

The next morning, we were up at sunrise, had breakfast, and went down to the boat to start another day of Sailfishing. Again, we had fish on within 10 minutes. Randy watched me for about 30 minutes to get the hang of it, and then we strapped her into the fighting chair and had a Sail on in about 5 minutes. I told her I was going downstairs in the air-conditioned suit and taking a nap. I was only down about an hour when I got on deck—Randy was beet-red and sweating profusely. I asked the guys how she did in Spanish, and they said she was a champ. She had brought 9 to the boat for release, and only two got off in the fight.

Randy and I caught about 20 sails between us that day, and that was plenty for a day.

The next day, we fished a half day in a different location, caught a few Dorado (Mahi Mahi) and a few Amberjack, and called it a day.

Coming back in that afternoon, one of the workers with a grin on his face asked me if I was ever coming back. I said, "Good Lord willing, I'm sure I would." He said, "Señor, if you make it back, will you please send Señorita Randy"

It was in Spanish, so Randy asked me what he was saying. I told her the guys wanted to see her go swimming again. You can imagine the look I got.

I mentioned to y'all in an earlier chapter that I was working on going down with Stormin' Norman, but before I could get him down there, they found he had very advanced prostate cancer.

Unfortunately, Norman never made the trip, but I would have loved to have fished with one of our most famous modern-day generals.

Chapter 17
The Red-Legged Baptism

A South Texas Bubba's Trial by Fire in Spain

I wasn't long into my consulting career when I found myself on a plane bound for Spain, surrounded by old money and older habits. This wasn't some typical business trip—it was a $20,000-per-head, high-dollar hunting expedition for Red-Legged Partridge and Driven Pheasants. The kind of getaway where leather gloves, silver flasks, and quiet butlers came standard.

I was just there to escort. Eight of them, all seasoned bird hunters from South Carolina, bred on Bob White Quail and bourbon. Most were in their sixties. I, on the other hand, was in my late twenties—a Bubba from South Texas. And this was the late 1980s. These men weren't just hunters; they were gentlemen with generations of sporting legacy behind them.

We met at the Admirals Club at Dallas-Fort Worth. Shined boots. Sport coats. Southern drawls that rolled like molasses. I kept my confidence close and my mouth shut. When boarding was called, we took our seats together—First Class, upper level.

The flight to Madrid was about eight hours, and I'll admit, the service made me feel like royalty. For a boy who'd grown up with dirt under his fingernails and gun dogs at his heels, this was a new world. Champagne flutes. Filet mignon midair. I was used to chewing jerky in a pickup truck between fence posts, not dining with sterling silver at 30,000 feet.

But when it came to bird hunting, I was no rookie. I'd grown up in the mesquite-dotted lands of South Texas, chasing Bob Whites over pointing dogs. I knew the rhythm, the tension before the flush, the grace of a clean shot. There ain't a better-tasting bird than those, and I'd bet my boots on it.

When we landed in Madrid, we were greeted like dignitaries. A caravan of luxury SUVs whisked us away to a lodge that looked like something out of a Hemingway novel. That first night was nothing short of decadent—an eight-course meal served with wines I couldn't pronounce and a floor show with dancers that could steal your breath if you weren't careful.

The next morning came early. We were lined up on a sun-drenched hillside, ten feet apart, with metal paddles stationed on each side of us to mark positions. At the whistle, a line of Spanish beaters began their slow advance from the horizon, pushing the game toward us with a cacophony of shouts and sticks against the brush.

It started with a whisper, and then the birds came.

Red-Legged Partridge, sleek and swift, flew like bullets. You didn't aim at them, you guessed their future and fired into it. These weren't lazy doves fluttering across a field. These were warp-speed missiles, and every shot had to be a prayer with gunpowder.

We had four to five drives that day, breaking in between with gourmet lunches laid out beneath linen-draped tables, with wine and laughter filling the gaps between reloads. It was a hell of a day, and for most of us, it was heaven. But not all of us.

From the first minute out of Dallas, one of the men, let's call him Mr. X, had been a walking storm cloud. He griped about the flight, the food, the weather, the birds, and even the beaters. Nothing pleased him. He was older, yes, but age doesn't excuse arrogance.

On the second day, the skies gave us a misty sprinkle. Any real hunter knows birds don't like wet feathers, and neither do we. But the hunt pushed on, wet boots and all. That night, we transferred to another lodge deeper in Southern Spain. The terrain changed. The air got sharper.

On Day Three, we faced a Driven Pheasant shoot. Picture this: we're at the base of a vast canyon wall. The pheasants are released from above, and they rain down like missiles, wind-flung and wild. For 45 minutes, we shot until our barrels burned. It was a hunter's dream, except, of course, for Mr. X, who found something new to whine about with every shell fired.

That night, I'd had enough.

I waited until most had turned in, then walked the hall to Mr. X's room and knocked.

"Come in," he grunted. He was propped up in bed, thumbing through a paperback.

I stepped in and squared my shoulders. I may have been half his age, but I wasn't half a man.

"Mr. X," I said plainly, "I don't know what your problem is, but you've been a royal pain in the ass since Dallas. Every damn day it's something. You whine, you moan, and you're dragging the whole trip down. Your friends are tired of it. I'm tired of it. And if you can't pull yourself together for the last couple of days, do us all a favor—keep your damn mouth shut."

He blinked at me. Said nothing. I didn't need a reply.

Something shifted. The final two days were blessed with sun-drenched skies, calm winds, and birds that flew as if the gods themselves had trained them. And Mr. X? Quiet. Respectful. Present.

One of the other men came to me that afternoon, clapping a hand on my shoulder.

"I don't know what you said to that old coot," he said with a grin, "but God bless you. It worked."

I just nodded. "Sometimes," I said, "you speak plain, and let God ride shotgun."

That final night was a celebration, wine flowing, cigars lit, stories traded under candlelight. There was laughter, friendship, and a bond forged through powder and grit. And when we boarded the flight home the next morning, Spain behind us, I carried something more than a suitcase.

I'd proven myself. To them. To me.

And I'd discovered something in the hills of Spain I hadn't known I had: the courage to stand up—even when standing alone.

How's that for my first international hunt?

And yes, Spain is a lovely place. Especially when it sharpens a man into something he didn't know he was becoming.

Chapter 18
The Last Circle

Do you remember the last paragraph of the China chapter? The one where we all placed our chairs in a large circle so they could ask me questions?

The first question came from the gentleman sitting on my left, the Secretary to the Governor of that province. His first question was simple, yet it struck deep:

"Tell me about your religion."

The lights in my head instantly went off. In that moment, I remembered him staring at the cross on the chain around my neck—the same chain I wore that night I was so sick, lying there while the doctor checked my vitals. Slowly, carefully, the doctor worked. As I recounted this memory through my interpreter, Wang, I could feel something greater unfolding.

I began explaining:

In America, we have many cultures. We have many religions. We have many different churches that people attend. But for me, it's always been about faith.

Not a religion.

Not a building.

Not a title.

A personal relationship with Jesus Christ.

I spent at least 25 minutes sharing just that, nothing more, nothing less. And I could tell they were deeply, genuinely interested.

There were many questions that night from both the men and the women. It took about four hours. By the time we finished, it was 1 a.m. I leaned over to Wang and said, "I'm bushed, I need to call it a night."

The very next morning, the first thing that happened, Jesus Christ was in the room with me.

He wasn't just there. I felt Him. He was speaking to me. He explained how He had placed the love and adventure in my heart long before I was born. Explaining how, while I was traveling the world, doing my work, He was using me, guiding me, to share His word in countries where many people didn't even know His name.

I kept visiting new places. New locations. And without fail, in every town, every gathering, every stop on the map, someone, some individual, would pull me aside and ask:

"You're different. Why are you so different from the others who visit?"

And every single time, I would smile. I knew the answer. And I shared it. Again and again. The answer never changed.

If you remember my Introduction, I said something important there. I suggested that I could not take credit for this book.

And I still can't.

All the credit goes to my Father.

But when I said "Father," I wasn't talking about my biological father.

I was talking about my Father and your Father in Heaven.

This isn't just the closing of a chapter.

This is the final circle. The final question. The final answer.

You now know why I was sent to that room in China, why the cross around my neck mattered, and why the questions kept coming.

And maybe now, you know why you picked up this book. Because this book, just like that circle of chairs in China, wasn't about me. It was never about me.

It was always about Him.

This is the end.

But this is not the finish.

This is your invitation.

Welcome to the circle.

Your question awaits.

And so does the answer.

With faith, always.

IT'S NOT ABOUT THE KILL